TAP DANCING

Harvey Price

Publisher: Harvey L. Price Jr.
Redmond, Oregon

ISBN: 978-0-9819220-8-9

Library of Congress Control Number: 2011914631

Back and Front Cover: Outside wall of a cabin in Idaho City, Idaho. Photo taken by author- 2008.

Appendix photo Guanay, Bolivia: © photograph by Yvon Maurice, Ottawa, Canada. Used with permission.

Appendix panorama photo Fort Davis, Texas: © Rick Gutleber (rickg@his.com). Used with permission.

Appendix University of Queensland maps/curriculum: © University of Queensland, Thomas Joyce (t.joyce@library.uq.edu.au). Used with permission.

Appendix Fort Davis photo: © photograph courtesy of Fort Davis Chamber of Commerce. Used with permission.

Printed by Minuteman Press, Olympia, Washington and bound by Phil's Bindery, Seattle, Washington.

FOR

My Beloved

ACKNOWLEDGEMENT

Each young boy's journey through life begins with him being influenced by those individuals who make the greatest impression on him, just as it is with young girls. The greatest difference between the two sexes at this point is that for the boys, laying in wait for them are the eons-old traditions and rituals of having to achieve their culture's predestined pathway into manhood, which will most certainly stunt their growth, character and potential. And certainly girls face obstacles for achieving their own potential, most of them fostered by the results of these same boys who have now completed these same manhood rituals

But if by good fortune, or chance, boys have had the opportunity to avoid this ritualized process into manhood and instead have had meaningful contact with men who are well-adjusted, civil and gracious citizens, then they, too, will become such.

In this author's case, I was extremely honored to have a series of men take my hand and begin ushering me into a world filled with temptations and potential pitfalls. Some of them may have been tainted by the ritual dance of manhood, but most were simply men of quality and character. They escorted and guided me through work, the community, education and lasting relationships. They were not tainted or flattered by pomp or ritual. They were simply good men. There needs to be more of them.

FOREWORD

Understandably, and very appropriately, much has relatively recently been and is still being written about girls and women. Books, articles, courses of study, degrees and entire university departments are devoted to their never-ending struggle to finally have universal equality; to have the most basic of human rights; about their suffering, abuse, neglect, torture, humiliation and mutilation; about their being dominated and only recently beginning to achieve their rightful place in all vocations and at all levels of leadership and ultimately about their becoming mature and responsible women

In stark contrast to this heroic movement is the sad and inexcusable role and undeniable responsibility that their male counterparts have played in this sorry heritage. Oral and written accounts abound regarding their conquests, insights, technological advances, discoveries and challenges. But it has been a glaringly tragic and one-sided legacy.

Most recently, as rightful emphasis has been given to the resurgence of women's rights and the importance of them beginning at the time of an infant girl's birth, there has been a noticeable decline in attention paid to young boys in this new and long overdue, social revolution. And inevitably, if civilization's bubble is ever to become steady and unwaveringly level, there must be more directed towards explaining and defining what a mature and responsible man should be and how he should behave.

Just as women's awful denial of rights and their ongoing abuse has prevented civilization from attaining a secure and lasting peace, so too has the equally dismal failure of boys becoming mature and faithful men. What follows is how three boys struggled to achieve this elusive goal.

Only time will tell if we will be able to do better. The reality and gnawing fear is that the world is still waiting.

APPENDIX

LET THE DANCING BEGIN

THE YUNGAS

ONE: GUANAY, BOLIVIA

If there was ever a birthplace or an environment that could easily stifle anyone's expectations or perspective or could just as easily ignite a spark of unquenchable rage and a desire to find and destroy those who forced him and his extended family to live in such a place, it was in the steep mountainside village of Guanay. (see Appendix: **Guanay, Bolivia**) While at the same time it could be a place of such awe-inspiring beauty and remoteness as to inspire the building of ancient empires.

The village was always being squeezed precariously on a shifting sand peninsula, between the Tipuani River and the unpredictable, often dangerously onrushing Mapiri River. Compounding its remoteness and isolation was its almost moment-to-moment, life-challenging existence at the base of some of the steepest mountain sides in the world. It would seem to an outsider to be the last place on Earth where someone of profound mystery and unparalleled tragic significance might originate.

The Tipuani River's usual cafe'au lait appearance was often streaked with darker shades of brown when heavier dredging and the associated blasting for gold was done 10-15 miles upstream around the village of Tipuani or when a heavy rainstorm eroded more of the steep volcanic hillsides in the nearby region. The larger Mapiri River drained a much larger area of the Cordillera Real, which included the high ridges of northeastern mountains of the Bolivia Andes. And its blue-grey color indicated that it was more influenced by runoff from their snow fields and glacial ice flows. In flood, the Mapiri could expand its shoreline to the homes of Guanay, threatening its townspeople with certain disaster. But life-altering events were the norm of everyday life in this settlement. That and isolation.

The only road in or out of Guanay either led upstream to Tipuani or downstream to Caranavi. If you continued following the road south, you would eventually reach La Paz, about 100 miles or ten hours ferried by the lorries which are often used in these parts as a form of public transportation or by the occasional, fully-packed bus. Once you depart Caranavi, however, one soon begins to climb the infamous Yungas Road or El Caminho de la Muerte, the Road of Death. In 1995 the Inter-American Bank declared it the "world's most dangerous road". And true to its name, both the humble and famous have lost their lives tumbling down its treacherous mountainsides. In 1961 a physician and the Executive Secretary of the Methodist Mission in Bolivia were both killed while trying to navigate it. And at the time this account begins, no major improvements had been made to lessen its danger.

The lush and fertile mountainside soil in the area did provide some additional, economic promise for the citizens of Guanay. And to do so, coffee bean cultivation and various, rural cooperatives were being developed and organized to successfully bring this commodity to market. But the placer mining for gold in the region's alluvial deposits still provided the most employment, especially for Tipuani and Chima, a mostly tattered hamlet further upstream on the Mapiri River. Mining for and acquiring gold in this region has been an ongoing quest for the last five hundred years, dating back to the Incan civilization.

Newcomers to the area quickly become hypnotized by its surrounding beauty. For as far as you can see vertically and horizontally there are the lush green mountainsides, some so steep you almost have to look straight up to view their peaks. And only where any previous or current mining has or is occurring do you see any change in this carpeted vista. It's in those areas that you see a disturbing, striated pattern underlying this same green carpet, but now it is merely perched on a couple feet of brownish-black top soil, which then overlays ten to twelve feet of reddish-orange volcanic outflow and under that is the most dominant color: that of the ore-bearing, whitish-gray quartzite. It is in this lowest level that the gold ore is extracted from... clumsily and dangerously, both for the workers and for those who live nearby. Deadly landslides are not uncommon, given the steep terrain and the insatiable appetite of all who are driven to find this ore.

But the Menani family's roots date back further than the mad rush for this glittering prize. That's because they are Aymara Indians; descended from a culture whose roots and language extend back more than two thousand years, predating the Inca's rise to prominence. Fritz and Yolanda Menani had two children before Inti was born. They were Isabella, age 5 and Pedro, age 3. Inti (which means "he who is bold" in the Aymara language) was born on August 12, 1992. And it is from that point that this story of such immense tragedy and sadness begins.

It was, by any account, a modest birth scene. After all, the Menani home still had just a partially framed stucco exterior, with only a small common living area, thatched river reeds for interior walls and a tin roof over its two bedrooms. Scattered in the backyard were a couple of metal sheds and a fenced-in area for their ten laying hens and an older, cranky rooster; and one smaller area for three pair of guinea pigs and their offspring. Most of the other homes in the community were two-story stucco's, but the Menani's initially spent most of their money getting a larger piece of property instead of building a bigger home right away. It was a work in progress, which was the case for most of Guanay.

Guanay's streets were essentially unpaved and strewn with bits of gravel and the ubiquitous whitish-gray rocks of moderate size that mark the aftereffects of mountain erosion and mining in the area. In an attempt to lessen the drabness of the town's landscape, many of its citizens had planted Peruvian Pepper trees. They were especially prevalent along the Mapiri River edge, serving as a kind of natural dyke to prevent further erosion and flooding. But the Memani's lived closer to the Tipiani River side of town where there are fewer trees. It was Yolanda's hope that they could begin planting a small orchard beside their vegetable garden soon.

As Fritz was able to earn some extra Bolivianos at work through bonuses, he would purchase additional wood beams and planking for remodeling the main house. Earning extra money was essential because his job as day-shift foreman at the Tipuani gold field doesn't usually provide for anything more than subsistence wages. The long-haul truck drivers make more than he does. And he used to drive, as well, until his accident four years ago when he was forced off the dirt roadway between Caranavi and Guanay by another truck passing in the opposite direction. That accident broke both his legs, and he was never able to shift gears easily or safely after their healing. But because of his excellent work record and ability to get along with all the other workers, the company's Vice-President of Operations approved the mine supervisor's recommendation for him to become a foreman when the previous one left for another job.

All in all the Menani family was relatively stable and secure. And it was considered a blessing when Yolanda became pregnant with Inti. The entire family anxiously awaited his arrival; so much so that it can never be said that Inti was neglected or unwanted. If anything, he was doted on from his first breath that August day in the Memani home, where he was delivered by the town's midwife with the entire family in attendance.

TWO: INTI'S FORMATIVE YEARS

From the moment Yolanda was first able to hold and cuddle Inti, the first thing she noticed was when he looked at her; it was a steady gaze, almost unblinking and purposeful. He didn't wail or whimper as often or as loud as Isabella and Pedro when they wanted to be fed or were uncomfortable. He was almost stoical about his needs or any discomfort. Whereas, her other children would indicate almost immediately when they were chilled or too hot or more often when they had soiled their bedding or swaddling clothes; Inti would maintain an almost monastic silence. This initially was so much of an issue that she had to make sure she and Isabella would check him regularly due to his soon developing skin rashes or scalding. But even when a rash did develop or he had scalded, these irritants did not prompt any noticeable reaction.

His appearance was most notable for the more intense brownish coloration of his skin. It was clear to her that this trait was not something he inherited from her, and this was primarily due to her grandparents and parents both having had spouses who were urbanized Aymarans, which meant that they had acquired an admixture of Spanish ethnicity. That was not as much the case with Fritz. His parents had an almost unblemished Aymaran bloodline, and this was readily evident by his overall, deep brownish coloration. This was primarily due to his parents and all his ancestral family before them having remained on the Altiplano for countless generations. There was no intermarriage with Spanish or other European invaders or settlers in his family tree. In fact, Fritz was the first of his family to ever leave the ancient homeland for the Yungas or "down below" as his parents used to call his destination, before they both passed away.

Studying Inti, Yolanda sensed that it was as if from his earliest moments of life in this remarkably beautiful but dangerous part of the world, he was reclaiming his native heritage and was already making some kind of a statement. But, of course, at this stage whatever that was to be completely escaped her.

Equally as unusual, and as mentioned earlier, was his habit of having an almost pensive or analytical gaze. Over time, it became an unsettling behavior pattern for both Yolanda and Fritz. Heightening the effect of this was that his brow would almost become furrowed when he stared at them; the look would become so intense at times. Whereas, with her other two children smiling and giggling was something that came easily and rather quickly, with Inti it was delayed and almost mechanical. There was both a gravity and purposefulness about him that puzzled Yolanda and at times even caused her some concern. Being fundamentally happy and having an easy laugh were two of the major cornerstones for survival amongst the harsh conditions that had always faced the Aymara civilization. She sensed from an early age, Inti would struggle to attain either of these native traits.

Equally obvious about his overall appearance was

that he seemed early on to have an uncommonly large chest wall. And again, that physical condition was a hallmark of the Aymara who lived in a hypobaric and hypoxic environment at 14,000 feet elevation on the Bolivian Altiplano all those centuries. That was because the diminished dissolved oxygen concentration in their blood at that elevation and the staggering physical demands for her people to build, farm and exist at that elevation meant that physiologically and anatomically their bodies had to adapt and compensate to survive. Like a badge of honor and recognition of his heritage, Inti's chest wall was oversized from birth, and so it remained throughout his life. And accompanying this anatomical inheritance was another equally common one as well; that of his being noticeably short, which was another Aymaran trait. He was always to be shorter for his age than his siblings and most of his classmates.

Four other developmental indicators also set Inti apart from Yolanda's other two children. Both of these earlier children seemed almost precocious with their desire and ability to begin saying words. From the time they started cruising and taking their first steps this phase began. Another distinct marker that always amazed her and Fritz was how they seemed to quickly grasp and accept the usual parental perimeters and restrictions for young children's safety. They seemed to mimic what they were told to do and not to do. It was as if they had an uncommon ability to process and then repeat whatever they were told. It was like generations of evolution was preparing them for being stewards of the oral tradition; passing on their family and clan's history to others. And by the time they were one and half years old, both of them were speaking in understandable phrases, with a vocabulary of over 200 words.

Inti, on the other hand, appeared neither to understand nor even to want to accept any age-driven, developmental timelines. And he uttered only the most basic words up to the time he was over three years old; at a time when his brother and sister were both speaking in short sentences.

Rather than complain or ask for something, he would announce in a voice surprisingly echoing with tinges of authority, even at that age: "food" or "go outside"; but curiously, he never seemed to voice any complaints nor whine or cry. He was stoical and his needs were simple, direct and uncomplicated. He seemed to always know exactly what he wanted and how to get it.

Equally puzzling to both his parents was the way he interacted with Pedro. Even though three years separated them, once Inti could walk throughout their small home, he seemed to begin taking control of his older brother's activities. There never seemed to be any cooperative or festive playtime with Inti. He appeared to be uncommonly competitive at the moment he no longer had limited locomotion and could thereby extend his will and begin to control his environment.

This was to set in motion later on in his life the need to prove his prowess in many areas of daily life, from interaction with his peers on the playground or sports court to academics and in relationships with other boys and, most especially, with girls and later on with the women he met.

Overall, he seemed to Yolanda to pass non-stop through child's play and move directly into a more serious and troubling stage: that of controlling others in a purposeful and organized manner. Soon Pedro would escape the confines of their yard and go play with other children in the neighborhood. But being alone never seemed to bother Inti; he was quite comfortable being alone.

But she already knew enough about her children, to know that as they passed through various stages of growth and development that they would exhibit traits and characteristics that she would want to catalog and probably worry some about. It only seemed natural for a parent to fret and project a child's immediate behavior into the future. The tendency to stereotype each of her children from month to month was a habit she couldn't break. But it didn't interfere with her loving them dearly and uncompromisingly. She only hoped that Inti would be talking more by the time he was old enough to start going to school.

And in Guanay all the formal education that was available took place in their one room schoolhouse. It was located on the north side of town, facing its one park and recreational area. The one, paid teacher provided instruction for five grades, and the students were subdivided throughout the room accordingly. It could be a rather noisy environment when there was language drill for their Spanish classes, given that the overwhelming majority of the students had Aymaran parents, and they spoke a broken combination of Spanish and Aymara. For any of the students to advance further in their education, learning a more fluent Spanish was essential; both to speak and to write.

Along with Spanish, there were classes in arithmetic, printing and cursory writing, Bolivian history and geography, health and organized sports. Not all these subjects were taught at the first grade level, but each was introduced as the class and individual students appeared ready to advance. Much depended on the motivation of each student. Their advancement in education was driven by their individual desire to learn and, most critically, their ability to successfully complete the government-mandated curriculum. Very few students went on to further schooling after these precious, few years. Sadly, that was due to their families needing them to help provide income and the necessary labor for their own survival. Child labor was common and vital. Advanced education was a luxury few of them could even consider.

And because Isabella was eleven years old and Pedro was nine when Inti started school at the age of five, there were only to be three years that he had them as school mentors. Isabella was a good student and wanted to go on to Caranavi to further her education, but she was desperately needed at home. Yolanda's health had begun to deteriorate during that first year Inti began his schooling, and it was time for Isabella to assume more responsibility for kitchen and household duties. And soon enough, it would fall upon Pedro to quit as well and to begin earning a wage to supplement Fritz' earnings. His father's health was also becoming a factor in the family's welfare. His crippling truck accident was now causing him to develop a further limiting arthritis. No one, it seemed to Isabella as she had to contemplate leaving behind her aspirations of further schooling, escaped the grind of coping with a harsh daily life in these unmerciful mountains. Maybe they had majesty and wonder for those who drifted through as tourists or mining engineers, but to the day-to-day workers, it was all a matter of survival. Even her family's and their neighbors' innate ability to laugh and find humor in the mundane did not prevent moments of desperate sadness at the struggle needed to survive for most of Guanay's citizens. Life for Pedro and Isabella was to be no different.

On the other hand, Inti, from the moment he entered the classroom that first day, appeared to have found his place and the avenue he was destined to take, and for an outcome far beyond the comprehension of most who knew him. He became immersed in learning. He absorbed everything quickly and permanently. And almost immediately, Yolanda noticed that his personality became more expansive and outgoing. Those first five years of his life had been like he was in a cocoon awaiting his time to emerge transformed.

Each day he ran home after school was over, yelling "mama, mama, look what I found out today!" And after describing or showing what it was, he would invariable add, "Isn't it wonderful, mama." To her it was a wonder; her undersized, withdrawn and fixed-gaze little boy had awakened at last. And she would always reply, "Indeed, my son, this is just grand. Be sure and show me all you learn and tell me about all you see." And thus began a unique bond between the two. It gave an outlet for expressing the magic of discovery to one and a reason for dealing with life's daily struggle for the other. It was the equivalent of an almost sacred, confessional ritual; the pouring out by one, the intense and eager awaiting to hear by the other. Yolanda knew soon enough that this child of hers was destined to free himself from the confinement of the surrounding steep canyons of dashed dreams. Her youngest son had already begun to loosen those bonds from that first day at school.

But that didn't replace the daily rigors of living in Guanay. Firewood still had to be cut and carted, the garden still had to be tended, clothes had to be mended and meals had to be organized and prepared for this family of five.

There was an orchestrated rhythm to it all that never varied from the time Inti was born. And he became a puppet in its ritual just like everyone else.

Preparing him for the upcoming changes in the location for his continued education, once he had to leave Guanay, Inti and his family had long established the practice of having simple meals and making sure there were readily available food sources. Breakfast always consisted of pondero or poncito bread, which was softer for the children to eat, and some rice and sweet black coffee. Intermixed with drinking coffee, Yolanda would prepare coffee bean husk tea or the more traditional, but a more time consuming drink from their pepper tree berries. To do this she would have to spend considerable time rubbing the sweet outer part of the ripe berries together and then let this mixture set a few days. It was one of Inti's favorite drinks.

The children always came home from school for their lunch. Often they had chechera, a corn bread with a large bowl of soup, which could either have llama meat or a raw egg mixed in it, along with some rice. And for dinner there might be rice with hot sauce, potatoes or chuna, and planteen bananas. Coffee or tea was served with both of these meals as well. Milk, butter and cream were delicacies rarely available to them. It wasn't until Inti left for Carnarvi and La Paz that he was able to add them to his diet.

The evening meal was when the family was able to socialize and entertain each other with their adventures and discoveries of that day. And Inti never tired of hearing his father tell of how the gold was mined and the dangers and surprises that they encountered. He knew both his father and mother were brave and stout-hearted people. But he also knew that his future, even in those formative years, was not to be directly connected in any way to this place. And everyone else in the family knew this as well.

THREE: LEAVING HOME

Because Inti began his primary schooling at the never-heard-of age of five, he completed the next five year's material in no less a surprising manner. By the age of nine, he had mastered everything that his instructor was commissioned to teach during these primary grades. Inti, by special permission from the district governmental, educational offices was allowed to advance to the intermediate level, and the closest school to Guanay was located in Caranavi. But for his parents to allow this, he would have to board with an aunt, his father's oldest sister. She lived alone in a two story apartment building, just three houses up from the Caranavi airstrip.

By all accounts, it was not a move that Inti was eager to make. Despite his precocious nature, he still loved his family very much and the thought of separating from them caused him regrets that lasted a lifetime and eventually led to consequences of an unimaginable toll. Poverty, and his family's struggle to cope with it, brought with it a visible handicap as well as an indefinable and lifelong longing. In Inti's case, even at his youthful age, it set in motion a desire to have companionship... however brief or impersonal it was to become. As the years passed, the void of his not having his family around him in those formative years led to his seeking shelter and conquest wherever he could. In short, it was to define his particular choice of a dance rhythm and style that would usher him into his own personal, ritualized quest for manhood.

And certainly, he had no idea of the choices available to him... or of the ramifications and consequences associated with each. Likewise, he had no grasp where this potentially perilous progression of each individual's lifelong dance could lead him. In short, he had no idea that life is a dance. One first must learn a dance's particular moves, which is most commonly done during the years of adolescence. Then there follows the need to choose a dance partner, which is most often done during the time of early adulthood. This is followed by the critical time of deciding whether, as a dance partner, there is to be shared gracefulness or complete dominance and its associated awkwardness. This would evolve in the ensuing adult years. And finally there would be the decision of which final dance style best suited you as an individual or as a couple. This is the most mature and defining period. Here, one either achieves or forgoes maturity. It's all a matter of deliberate choice and refining necessary skills. And it began for Inti that day the bus dropped him off at his aunt's home in Caranavi.

But certainly none of this was on his mind as he got off the bus and met his aunt Maria. She had been widowed two years previously, when the two ton lorry her husband drove was edged off the road as he was returning home from a trip to La Paz. Because the downhill traffic has to yield to those coming uphill from the Yungas, those vehicles have to move to the outside edge of the roadway. In a matter of seconds, once his truck was given an almost imperceptible nudge, his outside tires began to slip off the loose rock and dirt roadway. And in an instant it tipped and flipped over and over as it cascaded down the sheer cliff face into the dry stream bed three thousand feet below. Presumably knocked unconscious in the repeated rolling, it was everyone's opinion that he never knew when he struck the bottom of the canyon.

And with Maria having had scarlet fever as a child, which left her unable to have any children, following the tragic death of her husband, she was left essentially alone, with only Inti's family to claim as rarely-seen relatives. Truly excited about being asked to house and care for Inti, she enthusiastically welcomed the opportunity to have him in her home.

"Welcome to Caranavi," she called out, as he staggered off the last step of the bus. His legs were not long enough to gracefully step down to the ground, especially while at the same time holding his only luggage, a large nylon-webbed bag. It was filled with all the clothes he owned and some worn-out books and schoolwork notebooks he was able to acquire from his teacher who had kept them out of amazement at his intelligence. "And watch that last step; it's the highest," she added holding out her oversized hand as she steadied him.

"It's so good to see you!" she exclaimed, as she enveloped him in a long and loving hug. And aside from his own mother, somewhere deep inside, Inti knew at that very moment, that this genuine show of selfless affection was probably going to be one of the few he'd ever know in his life. Even then, he was feeling more and more disconnected from those around him. Possibly it was because of his advancing so effortlessly in school that he was aware of this at such a young age. Or maybe it was his having to travel alone to attend school away from his family and schoolmates. Or maybe it was something else; something that resides in each of us: that realization that our deepest self almost prefers isolation and transient commitment as a protective mechanism. Loneliness is the norm. Long term attachments are the exception, a sign of mental weakness. Too few people in anyone's life will selflessly reach out to you, love you, protect you and ask almost nothing in return. And if you are not careful, a disconnectedness and manipulation-prone outlook will develop and can become an invisible barrier to all who seek to reach out and touch you.

Shaking off these odd and fearful thoughts, he reached around her and squeezed her back with all the strength his undersized arms would allow.

"Thank you, Aunt Maria... for being here," he replied in an almost prayer-like whisper.

"Of course," she replied. "Now, come on. Let's get you something to eat and then get you settled into your new home for your next seven years!"

And thus began Inti's journey toward getting his baccalaureate degree. The first three years involved the intermediate schooling, which for him was almost a review of what he had mastered during his first five years in Guanay. And because he had come from out of town, it was that much harder for him to make friends. The cliques of school chums had already been well established, and his diminutive size and precious manner did not open many doors to friendship or companionship. In fact, what it did invite was a disturbing onset of bullying.

It began innocently enough with minor schoolyard taunts and avoiding choosing him for any games or sporting events. And his shyness around girls did not lessen the progression of this all too common activity. Often, the gang of instigators, when not pointing out his ineptness with kicking the soccer ball would shift to rounding up a couple of their girlfriend comrades and have one or two of them pretend to cuddle up to him and make suggestive remarks. It would serve to humiliate Inti, but his inner fortitude did not allow him to show any outward sign of being embarrassed. Instead, he would smile and pass it all off as some kind of joke. And this only emboldened his tormentors further. It was a vicious cycle that only began to lessen when he entered his secondary education years. It was these four years, the secondary cycle, which were the most formative for him. And as with his primary cycle, he quickly convinced his instructors that they were wasting his time during the first years of the secondary instruction, which consisted entirely of integrating what had been previously taught. Within a year of this program, he was advanced into the last two-year cycle, skipping an entire year, in which he was allowed to specialize in his two favorite subjects: physics and foreign languages.

And during these last two years, his relationship with his aunt took on its most far-reaching importance. She became his sole confidant. It was to her that he shared his innermost aspirations and fears. Sworn to secrecy, she never divulged any of what she was told to anyone, and he sensed that she would faithfully honor and respect what he shared with her. Included in his confidences were his bold plans for the future, such as wanting to go on to the University of Bolivia in La Paz to study physics and French... of all languages. He hoped one day to travel to France, where he would complete his studies and then live either in Paris or North Africa. It surprised her to hear of such hopes, but she never tried to dissuade him. In fact, there was such a determination and passion in his expressing these plans that she dared not do so.

Soon after these decisions were made, his aunt asked him one day, "Why physics and French? Was there any special reason you chose those subjects... especially French? Nobody speaks that around here... or anywhere else that I know about."

"Well," he replied, "I chose physics mainly because I'd love to see how things come together to form all that we see: the sun, trees, our rivers, you... me. And how each of them really works... both together and separately; and finally how they come apart."

"What do you mean, 'come apart?'", his aunt then pressed. "That seems dangerous to me."

"I guess I mean how things decay, explode or disappear."

"How did you ever come to seriously consider all that?"

"Probably by listening to my father tell about how they dynamited the mountain sides in search of gold, and how exciting it was to sometimes hear their explosions echoing in our valley. It all fascinated me, and now I want to see how it all happens."

"Ok," she reluctantly conceded. "But what about learning French; what gave you that idea?"

"I've read that some of the earliest scientists were French and the pictures I've seen in books of Paris makes me want to go there one day to study. But to do so, I'll have to learn French."

"Does anyone at your school know or teach any French?" she asked in growing amazement at her nephew's obvious thought-out reasons for his ambitious educational goals.

"No one actually teaches it as a course; but there is a biology teacher who has learned some basic French, and she has said she will try to help me as much as she can."

And with that conversation, his aunt was satisfied that his determination and justification for what he wanted to do were good enough for now, but then some days later he confided to her a more disturbing secret. It was then he tentatively and guardedly began to confess his interest in girls in his classes, but he was still too shy to approach any of them, other than to just say "Hi" or answer one of their many questions that he was always being asked, due to his remarkable grasp of the material presented in class or in the laboratory. And it was during the last year of his secondary studies that the bullying stopped as well. His aunt had always told him it would; that he would just have to be patient. This change seemed to coincide with his being approached more often by the girls in his classes.

And finally there was the matter of religion. His confessions about this matter were the only ones that shocked his aunt and caused her some discomfort and redoubling of her conviction to say nothing to anyone about what she was being told. Aside from Catholicism, the dominant religion throughout the region, there were scattered attempts by various Protestant church groups, namely Methodist, Quaker and generic Pentecostal missionaries who worked or passed through the area who attempted to convert the Yungas inhabitants. Inti voiced little interest in any of them to his aunt.

To him, they lacked a fiery conviction and a social relevance to address the poverty and emotional longings that he was personally experiencing. At this point in his life, he was an agnostic, something his aunt was totally unfamiliar with or unable to grasp. Her life of loss, day-to-day subsistence and hopes for a better life after this one compelled her to have an ever-present faith, expressed simply as "God's will be done". Inti was far from accepting that as his life's guide. He needed more. And nothing in his first fifteen years provided that. His search for meaning and purpose were now ready to advance beyond Caranavi to La Paz, and he ran home from school after graduation his last day with a Letter of Admission to the University of Bolivia. He was to begin his studies there in two months. And these two months were to be the last he'd ever spend in the Yungas. His determination and future were to lead him far away from these roots and his beloved aunt.

FOUR: UNIVERSITY STUDIES AND BEYOND

The bus ride to La Paz from Caranavi was one that Inti had always longed to take but had never had the opportunity or money to do so. His full scholarship to the University allowed him the funds to travel back and forth to his home at least twice a year. And despite his father telling him about the dangers and wonder of El Camino de la Muerte, the Road of Death (see Appendix: **Bolivia Yungas Road**), he was extremely excited at last to be traveling up it. And going uphill to La Paz, those traveling downhill were obligated to yield the right-of-way to his bus. All in all, it was an exciting initiation to his upcoming college education. And having just had his sixteenth birthday in August, he now felt like he was about to begin fulfilling his destiny. Unquestionably, these were amazing thoughts for such a young person to be having.

Never having ridden on this road before, he was stunned to see the various transition zones along the way. As they left the Yungas' deep valleys they passed through the more fertile coffee plantations, and then into the dense, drier shrub vegetation that clung to the increasingly rocky outcrops. With this changeover, there was a shift from predominately volcanic soil to solid granite walls; and in this transition the roadway became progressively narrower and steeper. Finally, they entered the highest altitude zone where there was essentially no vegetation. The view was such a sharp contrast to the region around his home. The overpowering vistas were limitless... in all directions. They included snow-capped mountains jutting above the desolate tan-brown, lower mountain range. Coupled with the cloudless, deepest blue sky he'd ever known, he experienced for the first time in his life, a sense of awe. He had the sensation he was being transported to the very top of the world. And, indeed, the highest motor-accessible roadway in the world was just south of his location about a hundred miles.

Then the most remarkable sight of all came into view as his bus topped the ridgeline, and he could see the full expanse of La Paz below him. Spread out over 1,200 square miles was the urban sprawl of this remarkable city, which although in a bowl, was situated at an elevation of 11, 975 feet. He could easily see how there might be over two million people living there. The dwellings spread across a massive bowl, from the top of one side to the top of the other, finally spilling over onto the Altiplano. It was like a huge flat area, once overflowing with countless homes and buildings that were suddenly sucked into this massive, bowl shape. Some buildings were so precariously perched on the steep hillsides they looked like collapsing at any moment was immanently possible.

The sky had a mid-summer haze which was overshadowed by the massive mountain to the city's southeast. There, brooding and ever-aware, staring down on the city was Illimana, a three peaked, 21,000 foot-high monster. (see Appendix: **La Paz**). It seemed to set a tone for the city, and remained a constant reminder to Inti that

24

something or someone always over-shadows you, looking over you, watching your every move. And it was at that moment he became aware of the ever-gnawing cold, something he had never experienced living in the Yungas. Combined, this mountainous setting and the chilled atmosphere began to kindle a kind of deep-seated paranoia that shaped many of his decisions forward. He was excited to be entering this remarkable city, but he was also impressed by the precautionary premonition this winding, hazardous journey and the brooding vista outstretched before him signaled.

Despite the University's student body having more than 39,000 students, upon his arrival that February 4, at the edge of the sprawling campus, he felt no anxiety. This was just the place and challenge he had longed for all the years he lived in Caranavi with his aunt. His first year's classes and all those that followed would always be in session from February to November. Characteristically, even upon his first seeing the campus, he hoped he could get a teaching assistant job as soon as possible for summer school in December and January.

And unbeknownst to him, with all he was experiencing in those first moments and days, his life-long dance lessons were also about to begin. The scholastic work at the Technological School campus was to become the challenge he had hoped it might be. Mixing chemistry, biology and physics lectures and laboratories together, along with his formal introduction to French was to fill most of the expanding void in his young life.

Still remaining were his individual dance lessons, beginning with Lesson One: The Waltz. This is the most elegant and sedate of all the dance routines that any boy who eventually achieves or earns the title of being a man will start with. The dance steps are relatively simple and do not require that your partner become too personally involved. It's a more exploratory kind of dance. You're getting to know your partner, and she you. There is no intimate touching involved, nor should there be. This is normally the beginning of that delicate process. And it involves much more than just the straightforward act of dancing.

Obviously, bear in mind that this rudimentary process of leaving childhood and adolescence will rarely begin in a ballroom-like setting. But wherever it begins, the process is the same. Basically, it entails those first, furtive attempts to become better acquainted with the opposite sex. But that is not to say that this is the only milestone that young boys must pass through for them to begin the long and mostly artificial and culturally-based journey into what is the locally accepted definition of what it takes to be a "man". Manhood, for all practical purposes and in most cultures, arises out of a fictional image or misrepresented social status. It is by and large a figment, a cultural deception, which is forced on young boys.

Becoming a man, as it is to become a woman, should be the one, true journey of a lifetime. And for Inti, the process of deciding which path he was going to take, be it toward the culturally-defined ideal of manhood or toward becoming a mature, self-aware and compassionate man now lies ahead. And for every boy, this choice begins with this first dance-like process. Whether it starts with his having to hunt for food, endure cruel hardships, display a sense of bravado in hazardous situations or teeter awkwardly during those first, close encounters with the opposite sex; or significantly more important to society, whether he takes the necessary risks and makes the awesomely difficult and lonely decisions to stand apart from this infantile game of pseudo manhood: that is the most fundamental decision any boy will make as he leaves childhood or adolescence. And this process will become an unavoidable addition to the scholastic curriculum that Inti will soon be undertaking.

His class work was challenging that first semester, mainly because it included having grueling laboratory assignments. What little practical class time he had in Caranavi was very basic and limited by the minimal amount of equipment the school was able to purchase. However, he wasted little time in catching up with other students and then began his remarkable ability to master and amaze his instructors and professors. Whether it was zoology, qualitative chemistry, or introductory physics, he soon was at the top of each class by mid-semester.

And because he was to live in a dormitory on campus for the first four years at the University as part of his scholarship, he began to make more friends than at any other time in his life. His youthful appearance and being two years younger than his fellow freshmen did not hamper many of his classmates wanting to know and be around him. Everyone who spent time with Inti recognized soon enough his quickness in grasping challenging classroom material and then in integrating what he learned into everyday life.

High on his list of things to start doing as soon as his studies would allow it was to begin investigating La Paz. Its huge size, rather than intimidate him, only intrigued him the more. Soon after arriving, he was able to purchase a relatively intact, used bicycle, which he used to head off in a different direction each day that he had the time to explore. Initially, he reserved most of his free time for checking out the cafes and sidewalk coffee bistros. Soon thereafter, though, his favorite place to visit in all La Paz was the Museum of Natural History.

And on one particular Sunday he was able to hitch a ride with a fellow classmate up onto the Altiplano where he saw Lake Titicaca for the first time. The lashed reed boats intrigued him, as did the people who lived fulltime at that altitude. And once up there, for him to see the ruins of the pre-Inca civilization, the Tiahuanaco, along with the rudimentary dwellings that his fellow Aymaran's lived in gave him both a surge of pride and the first hint of the injustice they experience daily. As time went on, he began wanting to address the wrongs that had been heaped on his people for countless generations.

In the meantime, his nuclear physics studies expanded with each new semester. Course titles beyond the rudimentary, freshman physics classes began to open up the Universe to him. As examples, he took a maze of undergraduate courses, sometimes two or three a semester in classical mechanics, electricity and magnetism, vibration and waves, statistical physics, quantum physics, physics of energy, general relativity, astrophysics and string theory. And then as he advanced to the graduate level, he began working towards his PhD, bypassing the requirement for a Masters Degree beforehand, due to his outstanding comprehension of the material.

He began his graduate studies with courses in relativistic quantum field theory, atomic and optical physics, neural networks, plasma physics and nuclear and particle physics. And when all that was completed, he began the work on his thesis, "The Growing Peril of Spent Nuclear Waste and How Best to Neutralize Its Long-term Potency". And because of France's vast dependency on nuclear power generating facilities scattered throughout the country, when the physics staff at the Sorbonne University heard of his thesis and of his outstanding academic record, along with his having four years of concentrated French language study, they offered him a full scholarship to finish his doctoral thesis at their institution. And their tentative plan was to eventually offer him a post-doctoral appointment there.

Three developments during these five years of living in La Paz deserve mentioning for what was to later become Inti's dance sequencing. These three permitted him to hasten though the normal progression of dance lessons and arrive at what was to be his signature one in a shorter period of time than occurs with most individuals. For the vast majority, they dodge and grasp frantically onto peer-driven expectations as they migrate into their individual society's unforgiving and rigid manhood rituals. The rare exception is the individual who escapes this cultic carnival and manages to develop socially outside of it and moves on.

The first of these more intimate explorations in life involved Inti's direct attempts to find some kind of lasting friendship or companionship with young women his age. Any previous attempts were and clumsy and immediately vaporized, aside from his adoring relationship with his mother and aunt. His high intelligence did not correspondingly translate into an equally charming disposition when it came to meeting and dating complete strangers. He had no idea of socially acceptable timing or the topics of conversation which would make his date feel at ease and comfortable in his presence. And unfortunately, he seemed unaware when he had been insensitive or insulted her. Repeated attempts at being humorous and gregarious were usually met with a quizzical look and silence. And this whole process was even made worse when he was in a group of couples enjoying some outing or spending time in a local coffee house or pub. His level of self-consciousness only grew because of this ineptness. It soon became obvious to him that word was being spread about the huge campus that he was a miserable escort or date to any function. As a result, he progressively became a more solitary individual; shunning both female and male associations... other than those he had contact with in his coursework or teaching assignments, particularly in laboratory settings. And almost inadvertently, this social misfit status led him to seek company in seedy bars and in alleys and side-streets. A darker side of his nature was being exposed by this lack of socialization skills.

This shunning led to Inti's next exploratory venture. But before describing it in some detail, it should be noted that he was raised in a Roman Catholic family and was to attend Mass on a regular basis both in Guanay and with his aunt in Caranavi. And upon the rare occasion, he even participated in the Sacrament of Confession, but by the time he took this next developmental step, he had not been either to Mass or to Confession for almost five years. And his fruitless attempts at establishing some lasting relationship with a woman only led him to search for answers along a totally different avenue and within a vastly different religion.

It wasn't as if he was a seeker of any truth that might be residing in what to him seemed the irrational, spiritually-oriented realm of organized religion or that he was on a quest to find the meaning of life. His scientifically-oriented mind was comfortable with the limited existential exploration he was undertaking through his studies. He considered having faith or trust in something unprovable or incapable of being measured by trusted analysis foolish and a waste of time. And the meaning of life held no fascination for him. Seeing his parent's and the citizens of Quanay's daily struggle convinced him there could be no lasting significance in their living. He was convinced that only by freeing them from their constant battle for survival could their lives ever have lasting meaning.

Furthermore his attendance at church had been something he did out of his deep respect for his family and aunt. But since being away from them, he became convinced he was indifferent to expressions of religious devotion. If others wanted or needed that in their lives, he rather condescendingly excused it as a somewhat harmless ritual. But he also knew, through the awareness of his family's violent and tragic Aymara history, that religion, while it could be a force for peace, too often had been used as a justification for conquest and war.

There was a power inherent in its rites and beliefs that he did admire. And he was ready to see if exploring such in other religions might give him that edge with his aborted attempts at romance. It was a backdoor approach. By outwardly appearing to become a faithful follower of some creed, he hoped to have at least a temporary relationship with a woman. Convinced this was a logical course to take, he decided to give this venture a dedicated effort.

And as sometimes happens in life's search for avenues of change, not more than three blocks from where his apartment was located, the one he had been able to rent once he started his post-graduate studies, there was an

Islamic Mosque. Further, he knew a couple of fellows in his physics tutorials that attended it. Although he only knew them by sight and brief discussions about their studies, nothing about religion had ever been mentioned between them. He had just overheard them speak of their going to Friday services at this same Mosque. Over time, and driven by his progressive preoccupation of needing to succeed with a romantic relationship, he asked them one day where their religious services were held. Graciously, they briefly described their place of worship and invited him to attend the next worship service.

Tentatively, and quite out of character, for someone who had become so in command of higher education's challenges and of the concepts and theories of the most complex field in all science, he prodded himself to climb the steps into the Mosque the next Friday. He had done so immediately following the call of the muezzin for Dhuhr, the noon prayer.

Upon entering the mosque, he noted that it appeared to be a converted warehouse or business of some kind. It was a three story building, with offices and possibly some small classrooms on the first floor. The second floor was where he was directed for the daily prayers ritual. It consisted of a massive room, which had been painted entirely white, giving it the appearance of a place where one might find a soul-cleansing peace. Against the backdrop of the harsh, cold and denuded dusty browns surrounding La Paz, it was a welcome change for Inti. And he was surprised to see that there were only men in the room at this time. This was his second surprise.

Oddly, given that his initial reason for this dubious quest was for another way to meet and find some finality in his relationships with women, there was something about this all male congregation that seemed to empower and embolden him. Further, the longer he bowed in this company and the more times he did so, he began to sense that being in this setting granted him a fundamental justification for the way he was beginning to feel about all women. His thinking and emotions were becoming centered on his wanting not to just meet and successfully court them, but he now wanted to dominate them as well.

Being in this environment, as often as five times a day, was to become the comforting retreat he needed and was seeking. He came away that first day with a serenity and boldness he'd never known before. An outwardly indiscernible restlessness was disappearing.

And in subsequent visits to the mosque, he was able to listen and question the Iman about how the Shria Law applied to the daily lives of Muslims. It only fed a further interest and a sense of longing inside him. And by the third month of his attending both the call to prayers and classes given by the Iman and others, he decided to convert, or "revert", as his soon-to-be fellow Muslins would say to him in their eagerness for him join them in their Islamic faith. The process was simple but held great significance to Inti. The day he reverted was one he never forgot as long as he lived. The ceremony was simple and solemn. He was asked to embrace Islam as his faith and repeat the following words of the "Shahada", the testimony of faith, with firm conviction and belief: "Ash-hadu an la ilaha ill Allah. Wa ash-hadu ana Muhammad ar-rasullallah." (I bear witness that there is no deity but Allah. And I bear witness that Muhammad is the Messenger of Allah.) This was soon followed by his taking a symbolically cleansing shower in a room especially reserved for this purpose within the Mosque. It was to symbolize that he had cleansed himself of his life previous to this conversion and that all other professions of faith were now cast aside.

For all his life, he had stood apart, even within his beloved family. His high intelligence and lofty ambitions kept him detached, and he often appeared aloof. Now, at last, he had brothers who cared deeply about him and his pathway in life. He had become a believer. And sadly, he later recalled, he made such a radical about face that he never returned home to see anyone in his family. His attitude of mental superiority and conformity to the way of Islam, and its brotherhood, altered his attitude entirely about his ancestral roots and immediate family. Now all that was left was to apply this same energy and new life to establishing a lasting relationship with a woman of his liking. He was certain that would only be a matter of time now.

It was only a month later that he got the letter addressed to him from the Admissions Office of Sorbonne University. In it was an invitation to finish his PhD in nuclear physics at their institution. Along with that there was a promissory note of one round–trip ticket to Paris, France and back to La Paz to have a perfunctory interview. But the letter also indicated that none was necessary. He could just come in one month already packed and ready to continue his thesis development.

Sitting down to keep from falling, he let out a long sigh and whispered, "At last. The future is mine…"

THE GLASS HOUSE MOUNTAINS

FIVE: LANDSBOROUGH, QUEENSLAND

From 1770, when Captain Cook and his crew first spied the Glass House Mountains, which reminded him of the large glass furnaces (glasshouses) in his native England, this region of Australia has held a lingering fascination and an almost indiscernible mystique for the Aboriginals since well before recorded time. They were so impressed with the region that they named a nearby, ancient settlement of theirs, "Caloundra", which means, "the beautiful place" in their language. (see Appendix: **The Glass House Mountains**)

The nearby Coral Sea, bordering this area's eastern landmass, is a remarkable greenish-blue, stretching in either direction into the distant horizon. The sea's touching the pristine white, sandy shoreline of this part of Queensland is a marriage of an ancient, undisturbed land with a restless sea. The shoreline marks where a tenuous treaty between man and nature exists. In either direction there lies the potential for adventure, riches and danger. And the sea offers a ready food supply and on most days visual comfort; all the while ominously and silently reminding anyone who will pay close enough attention that those who dare live within its reach, the hazards of violent storms or of the terrible aftermaths of earth's occasional massive upheavals are never to be forgotten.

Inland, there is fertile volcanic soil that nourishes countless varieties and shapes of trees, shrubs, birds and animals, most of whom are peculiar to this isolated land and nowhere else. Fruits and other foodstuffs of all sizes and descriptions grow in abundance here... from bananas, pineapples and passion fruit to macadamia nuts and sugar cane. The Blackall mountain range is filled with natural lakes and steep, waist-high grassy hillsides which house some of the world's most venomous snakes and spiders. All the while, the gum, bunya pine, beech and red cedar tree groves are filled with the calls and occasional sightings of various birds of paradise. It's an ancient landmass, which will entice anyone with both its beauty and its lurking dangers. And both these qualities shape the people who have tried for tens of thousands of years to tame and settle this land. It offers up its beauty for all to see. It likewise cautions all who come and stay to beware of its allure and secrets. And it's a haunted land, and all who try to tame it or live within its boundaries are touched by its magical powers.

But undaunted, the first white settlers to stay in this region, occupied and developed the town of Landsborough. Settled in 1871 and with the railroad line from Brisbane extended through it in 1890, the community soon became a bustling logging town. The town was named for William Landsborough, the first explorer to cross Australia from its northern border to its southern one. The original name for the town was "Mellum", which is an Aboriginal word for "volcano". One only has to look north to the Blackall

Range and south to the volcanic cores that dot the Glass House Mountain's landscape to know why they did.

But this is a different story, and it begins on August 12, 1982. That was when Colin Michael Kennard was born to June and Tobias Kennard in the Caloundra Base Hospital. At that time the town of Landsborough had a population of approximately 1,500 and had long since settled into comfortable passivity. Its last brush with history was during the Second World War when American troops encamped nearby and traveled through the area in route to the campaigns in New Guinea and the Philippines.

By the time of Colin's birth, the town was more of a bedroom community for those who commuted by train or car into Brisbane or the other cities within the Sunshine Coastal area of Queensland. But Tobias Kennard still worked in the small village. He was the owner of the Landsborough Pub, the largest building and the only hotel in town, located across the street from the train station. It had been passed down through the family for two generations, and it was expected that with the birth of Colin that he, too, would become his father's successor.

Adjacent to it are small shops, but no building in the community is as large or as recognizable as the hotel/pub. And nestled around the main street are the bungalow homes that were built over the years by workers in the forest, in the gold fields or on the railroad. It has a comfortable quality about it. Passenger and "goods" trains pass through on a regular basis, some occasionally stopping to load and unload passengers or freight; and after they depart, the low hum of a community which is determined to live on resumes, despite recent history and economic trends pushing population growth and prosperity further west to cities along the coastline.

Tobias kept long hours, having to fill in on a regular basis for individual work crew members which were either "crook", as the Aussies' say when someone is not feeling well or is just not interested in working a particular day or shift; or they were on holiday or having a vacation. He knew when someone was taking a personal day, rather than being ill, but his staff had stayed with the hotel for many years; and it was worth his filling in to keep them on and keep the customers happy and returning. He was known for being fair-minded and a good boss. And the community looked to his establishment as being the center of activities and celebrations on holidays and special occasions. Another source of increased business was that his hotel was across the street from the train station. This allowed occasional return customers from towns along the commuter line from Nambour to Brisbane to eat or spend the night.

All and all, this area of Queensland was ideal for someone to be born and raised in. The opportunities, beauty and loving support that were to surround and nurture Colin were limitless. It was a stage ready-made for success and happiness. The question that always remains is what dance steps will he choose to learn and which ones will he be destined to having to learn.

SIX: COLIN'S EARLY YEARS

June thought Colin's conception and birth were absolute miracles. At age the of 39 and Tobias 41, she was stunned when the General Practitioner she went to in Coulandra told her she was pregnant. Even her doctor was surprised, knowing June as long as she had and how hard she and Tobias had tried to conceive a child for so many years. Colin was to be their first and only child. And at his birth, from all appearances and movements, their dear son looked and acted perfectly normal in every way. No one could have wanted for a more loving and dedicated pair of parents. And so it was throughout his life.

His earliest development and childhood were highlighted by his ready smile and easy laugh. Without any doubt, he was a cheerful and fun-loving boy, right from the time he left his bassinet at the hospital. And although he had no brothers or sisters to play with, he made friends easily and kept them.

Throughout these years, June loved being a homemaker and helping her son and husband thrive. Her cooking was legend, and often she would make special dishes for the pub's Counter Lunch special, which was served each weekday at noon. Her curry and lamb dishes were so special that when it was posted on the next week's menu, people would drive out from Coloundra just to eat what she had prepared.

Colin began spending more and more time in the hotel when he was about seven. Before that, he was a kind of roving mascot. But when he reached that age, his dad put him to work doing small, odd chores like cleaning tables, sweeping and dusting the hotel lobby and hallways. However, that was not the main attraction for Colin... not even remotely. He was a sports fan... rugby; cricket; Aussie rules football, which is a kind of kick-pass-catch soccer game or "footy", for short; track; swimming and even basketball... the newest athletic event to make its way into Australian competition at that time. And the more he became involved in sports, the more both his mother and father began to notice a change in his manner and priorities.

His beginning dance steps were not waltz-like, as was the case with Inti. Instead, he began with a cross between the tango and the jitterbug. His bodily movements were fluid and graceful, perfectly coordinated and almost sinuous, while at the same time they could be carefree and yet balanced. He was developing into a model athlete, both in build and agility.

Early on, he began to excel at whatever athletic-type activity he tried. His successes seem to run a rather predictive sequence of acquiring the necessary advanced skill and strength, starting with cricket and progressing to Aussie Rules Football. At the same time, his mother noted that a certain overconfidence or cockiness was becoming a regular pattern of behavior. Even his ever-forgiving father began to notice the change. Whereas, there was once a carefree and engaging manner, they both saw it gradually being replaced with a strong desire to best others in all he did. It was a kind of one-upmanship that disturbed them. But his father reassured her it was just a passing phase. And to some degree she began to admit that she had probably jumped to conclusions. As he was introduced to surfing along the coastline near Coolum Beach, along with deep sea fishing with his cousin and family for marlin, he did appear to lose some of this irritating, competitive edginess. But unlike June, Tobias was thrilled at how well he performed athletically. He attended all his games, contests and events, and their bond became stronger and stronger.

And complementing this gradual change for the better was his deepening involvement with school studies. In Queensland Preschool or Kindergarten is taught within the Primary School framework. And at the age of five, he was enrolled in Preparatory School. And at age six, he entered Year 1 of his primary education. Unlike Inti, he was not precocious nor considered particularly bright, but he was perseverant and by Year 7 of his Primary School years, his competitiveness began to emerge, which compensated for his not being at the very top of his class intellectually.

And by the time Colin entered Secondary or High School in Caloundra, there not being enough students in Landsborough to even consider having one, he was beginning to collect trophies, medals and ribbons for his athletic prowess. He became the pride of that city and of his home town. His father had a display case built and placed prominently in the Hotel's bar area. Inside were newspaper clippings, photographs, and all Colin's prizes and trophies. He was fast becoming the hometown hero.

And again, unlike Inti, he never lacked for either girl or boy companions wherever he went or whatever he did. His popularity rose as his athletic accomplishments grew. His individual trajectory of dances had begun at an early age, as previously mentioned. Likewise, the manhood ritual began uncommonly early for Colin, due to his special physical abilities. If anything, it looked as if the accepted definition of manhood in his culture was going to bestow upon him this title well before many others his age; superior athletic ability provided that accredited pathway for some youngsters. Like jousting, hunting or preteen military-like academies, excellence in athletics bestowed upon a youngster the early mantel of acceptance into that sought-after title. Athleticism was becoming the late twentieth century's key to an early and assured passport into this often elusive club. It would seem to delay or even deny or prevent the usual, lifetime procession of dance moves toward any real chance of becoming a man, in the truest sense. And capping off this premature, elevated social status for Colin was that he was also considered the most handsome fellow in his high school graduating class.

Just the same, there is a hidden price to pay for someone who embraces the attitude of always wanting to best the next person you compete against or who you meet for the first time socially or who you even bump into in a casual way. The need to be seen as better than the person you just met or have as a rival will ultimately result in their developing a nagging sense of isolation. There is an insecurity buried in this obsession to always portray oneself as unbeatable and untouchable. And for Colin, a progressive sense of isolation led to its common companions: regionalism and parochialism. All this further haunted June. She knew that despite so many of her fellow countrymen and women displaying a similar reserve when confronted with international issues or foreign visitors, her recognition of this developing flaw in her son made her want to redirect him in some manner.

She knew the future belonged to those who looked beyond the shores of their own town, state and country. Armed with this awareness and resolve, she approached Colin one evening some months prior to his graduation from high school.

"Colin!" she called out as he came in the front door after a long swimming team practice, "I need to talk with you about something that I have wanted to tell you for some time now."

"Sure thing, mum," he replied, as he came into the kitchen and reached into a cupboard to get a glass for some ice tea. "What's up?"

"It's about your plans to go to University next year. Have you applied yet?"

"Well, not exactly…"

"What does that mean?, she asked, with a hint of exasperation in her voice.

"It means that I want to, but I can't seem to decide which direction to take. And to be frank, if I had my way I'd probably not go at all and just try to play footy for one of the major league teams… if they would give me a chance to try out."

"I figured as much," his mother sighed. "I knew if I let you just coast through this final year of high school that you would probably not apply anywhere. You and your dad! All you two ever think of is the next athletic event or the next sport you two will be attending or competing in. Your bedroom is so cluttered now with all your medals and trophies. But believe me, none of that will provide you with any kind of security, and you can be sure that assuming that our hotel business will always be there to support you is sheer fantasy. With the downturn in the economy we are having now and the skyrocketing costs of food and equipment we have to import, there is always the chance that we will have to declare bankruptcy. Your father just never talks to you about this.

"But to your favor, we began a savings account for you when you were born, and in the mid to late 80's, when interest rates were so high, we were able to triple and even quadruple our investments for your university expenses. And on that note, you might as well know, we have put nothing aside for our own retirement. Our one goal was to provide you the best education possible. And now I fear that you are being side-tracked into thinking that your athletic ability and good looks will get you whatever you want.

"And I'm sorry to have to be talking to you like this, but time is running out. You have to decide on a major and begin to apply yourself toward that goal. And most of all, you have to apply immediately to some Tertiary Admissions Centre. It's already April, and the university's school year begins in late February next year."

"I know. I know." was Colin's only response. It was quite evident by now that he was seeing and hearing a side of his mother that disturbed him. Only she could break through his façade of effortless athleticism, superficial mastery of social skills and general bon vivant. And he knew that at some point this conversation was bound to happen. He was cornered. She was the one person he was unable to impress enough or avoid. His dad hung on his every move and word. His mother weighed it all... and saw through him. She had been tolerant of his superficial successes up to that point, but he always sensed that she was not fooled. Having lost her own mother when she was quite young, a brother who was a laggard and a father who continually failed at a myriad of business ventures due to his inability to face the reality of never properly preparing for a career or developing a marketable skill, she had developed a sixth sense about someone in denial, procrastinating or developing an over-blown sense of their own self worth. In short, she knew when someone was being foolish or head-strong. He never heard her talk despairingly about anyone; but he always sensed that she knew more about his internal conflicts and fears but held back any comments... until now.

"What do you suggest that I do then, mum?"

"Decide here and now what you want to begin studying," she hurriedly replied. "You've always had high marks in English and Mathematics. You should take advantage of these natural abilities. And your ease of moving in and out of difficult situations, whether on a playing field or faced with an awkward social encounter indicates that you have the adaptability to potentially handle more complex issues and in settings that others of us would not."

"So?" he prompted.

"So... I think you should seriously consider applying to the University of Queensland for admission into their Economics program. You can take the commuter train from here on a daily basis, saving any expense for food and housing. Right away you can get a part-time job that will help with the annual admission fee of five to six thousand dollars."

"And then what?" he asked, shocked now by how well she had thought out the plan she was outlining for him.

"Then you see how far your diligent study and work takes you. For once in your young life something will not be easy. But if you try, I know you can successfully make it. And believe me, I will be there every step of the way. What do you say?

"What can I say? You are right. I know I have taken the easy path, ever since I was just a small boy. And you've known all along that I was doing so. You're challenging me now to make something of myself... apart from yours and dad's business.

"I'll take the train into Brisbane and go by the University's St. Lucia Campus tomorrow and see how I begin the process of applying for admission into their Economics program."

And with that, the two hugged each other tenderly, more so than either had ever known. His next dance routine was now to become more complicated.

SEVEN: UNIVERSITY STUDIES AND BEYOND

For all the ease with which Colin navigated through his childhood and adolescent years in school, sports and social interactions, that was certainly not the case with his introduction into University life. He tried to maintain a determined and positive outlook, meeting and greeting his fellow students and instructors with a hearty spirit, but oozing up and out through his pores were previously denied or suppressed feelings of, deep-seated loneliness and almost paralyzing insecurity. He had mastered the art of divulging just enough of himself to others, appearing confidently in control of his own personal life and displaying enough physical grace and mental alertness to keep his family, fellow students and primary and secondary teachers unaware of his deepest dreads. But the first weeks at the University of Queensland stirred these dormant and now expanding abscesses.

No one else he had known ventured anywhere near the University. Only he strayed so far from his previously coveted, comfort zone. His mother had challenged him. His father had supported him. And now he was alone and facing a desperately daunting future… alone.

Compounding the feeling of isolation was his

needing to travel by train back and forth to the campus each day. It gave him little to no time to interact with fellow students. Gradually and surely, his world shrunk. The days of glory were now well behind him.

And further adding to his sense of alienation and overwhelming challenge was the "Conditional Acceptance" he received for admission to the University. It was to be probationary due to his grades for classes in high school other than those in English and Mathematics. But his final grades in those two disciplines were so high the Economics Department Admissions Committee, in a contested but over-ruled vote in his favor, admitted him conditionally into the program. However, he had only one semester to prove his overall academic capability for this admission and to become unconditionally released from probation. For once, his athletic abilities and charm did not grant him unqualified entrance into whatever he chose to do.

But his mother was thrilled anyway that he followed through with the agreement they had. All in all, his father was puzzled over this development. He had wanted Colin to sign up for try-outs as a wingman in the local, semi-professional franchise football team and then eventually go on to play for Queensland's premiere team, the Brisbane team. Ever since their formation in 1996, when Fitroy's team merged with Brisbane's lackluster one, there had been slow but steady improvement in the team. Colin and his father were rapt followers and often attended their home games in the Brisbane stadium, the Gabba, which seats over 42,000 adoring and very boisterous fans.

That, and he hoped his son would eventually take over management of the Hotel. He harbored hopes that his son could turn the business around with his many contacts and friends in Caloundra. But neither of his not-so-secret desires for Colin were to be realized.

Instead, Colin had awkwardly chosen another pathway into his future. Reinforcing that, his first day at the University was bewildering, despite his having to interview multiple times at the Queensland Tertiary Admission Centre (QTAC) prior to February 16th, the day classes commenced. His being so overwhelmed was due in part to his commuter train arriving late in Landsborough that first day of classes. And then he missed his bus connection from the train station to the University as a result of the train being behind schedule.

In a frantic sprint across campus to the Colin Clark Building on the St. Lucia Campus (see Appendix: **Map of St. Lucia and Colin Clark Building**), he rushed breathlessly into his first day's Economic's class fifteen minutes after the lecture had started. Obviously seeing him arrive so late, the professor sighed at his suddenly barging into the auditorium and gave him the all-knowing look that the first failure of this semester had just arrived. He off-handedly motioned for him to take an empty seat at the back of the auditorium.

Thus began his formal education in a field that he had only the vaguest idea what it involved and how the class work would unfold. (see Appendix: **Colin Kennard's Bachelor of Economics (BEcon) Three Year Curriculum**) He had had little time to digest what was ahead for him. And as it turned out, he had to take at least 8 credits each semester; and all of them were in this one field of study. By the third year he had to declare a major within the field of Economics and then take seven courses in that major. The fourth year of his University studies would be in the Honours program, should he be fortunate enough and his grades high enough to be admitted. But all that seemed far, far into the future. Particularly that first day he dashed into the lecture hall.

His freshman year was grueling, and it only reinforced his isolation and loneliness. Not living on or nearby the campus sharply limited his opportunities to meet other students, and the friends he had in high school began to drift away... mostly because he was now a "University Student". It was a prejudice that puzzled him for the rest of his life.

And adding to that were the time constraints; there being so little leisure time left after his class work, commuting, studies and a part-time job as a real estate salesman for a couple of land developers. He got this job because there were burgeoning, start-up communities throughout the Sunshine Coast of Queensland, and buyers were flocking there from all over Australia and southwestern Asia.

And yet, given all this, his most striking challenge and eventual accomplishment that first year was his dogged perseverance with his studies and how with each examination he took or research paper he wrote, he began to rise in the standings of each of his classes. Initially, he did poorly in all of them, reinforcing what that professor's outward show of distain indicated would happen. But by midterm he was well into the eighty percentile of every class. And by the end of that first semester, he had a solid 94 percent in each of them, and his probation was lifted by the Tertiary Admissions Centre. At that point his professors began to watch him closely for signs of an unrecognized, exceptional student. And to reinforce this decision by the Admissions Centre, the Economics Department assigned him to an advisory professor, and later he was asked to be part of the peer-assisted study program for first year students.

Most gratifying to Colin was that there was a stipend for working with freshmen, which meant he could quit his part-time job and eventually begin to look for some residence near the campus.

This gave him more hope than he had had all year; mainly because there had likewise been no time during this first year to begin or sustain any serious dating. His high school girlfriend had moved to Victoria immediately after their high school graduation, and she had not answered any of his letters. And aside from some rather lame conversations in the Student Union Complex or after class with any students, he had not had any dates or chances for such the entire school year.

However, a stunning turnaround happened that first summer. Not only did he get the peer-assistance job, but his faculty advisor suggested that he move into a garage apartment behind his house just a few blocks from the campus. These were the opportunities he needed to continue moving forward. And as he was to learn time and again in his life, chance opportunities are not just random occurrences. They are earned. And they are earned when you are doing your best, without regard to who might be noticing or caring. It's an outgrowth of diligence and dedication.

Consequently, throughout the next two years Colin became a notable presence in the Bachelor's program. The tennis courts, rugby and Aussie rules football fields were across the street from the Colin Clark Building, and he began to have more time to participate in collegiate athletics. And living just off-campus, he slowly began to date. But it wasn't long thereafter that he met Jill.

It occurred one summer morning after his Freshman

Year. This opportunity initiated the second phase in his developing dancing skills towards achieving the character of a man or, more likely, in his continuing to follow the ritual pathway into manhood. It is the process of beginning to choose a partner. It most often occurs, as you would imagine, during the period of young adulthood, and its importance cannot be overstated. From here on, there are concrete and unmistakable signposts that define whether an individual becomes a sharing, loving, responsive and unselfish man. His ritual pathway, if left undisturbed, was to differ from Inti's. It is often labeled as being that of the provider.

It happened in mid-December, just one week before Christmas. Colin was gradually becoming more aware of his need to establish a regular exercise routine. Attempting to compete in team sports was frustrating, given his overall poor physical condition from his inactivity over the last year. Without consistent training, he knew he was asking for an injury. And as much as he used to feel that jogging was a waste of time, he was trying to establish a regular routine in the early morning to gradually build up his stamina and also possibly develop a commitment to continue it.

It was during his third week of trying to establish a routine time of day that he took the time to observe more thoroughly the surroundings, and to see whether there was anyone else exercising on the oval track. And to his surprise, there was another lone jogger. And over that week he noted the individual seemed to appear about the same time he did each day. Then on the Friday of that week, he had trouble with his shoe laces and had to stop to fix them, and that same lone jogger came running up to him.

"Are you ok?" she asked in a voice that to him seemed genuinely concerned; it was obvious right away that it wasn't just a casual, off-handed remark.

"Yes. Thank you," he replied while looking up to see someone who appeared to radiate both beauty and sincere concern. "It's my shoe laces. I've had these shoes since I was in grade 10, and they seem to be telling me that their time of usefulness is past."

"You have to be careful and not trip on this all-weather, cinder track. It can cause nasty scrapes and cuts on hands, elbows or knees." And upon seeing and hearing that he was ok, she excused herself and prepared to resume running.

"My name is Colin," he suddenly exclaimed, as if he didn't want this opportunity to arise and not pursue it. Suddenly, he had an uncommon chance to possibly know someone on campus.

"Hello Colin. My name is Jill."

Getting up after securely tying his shoe laces, he awkwardly stretched out his hand in an offer to shake hers. And as he might have predicted from her earlier stopping to inquire about his wellbeing, she did not hesitate and extended her right hand as well.

"Would you mind terribly, if I jogged along beside you for a while?" he cautiously added, brushing off his sweat pants, as he asked.

"No. That would be nice. I've noticed you running here for the last couple of weeks. You seemed rather intent on what you were doing. Are you just getting started on an exercise program?"

"In a way, I suppose. After this last year I have had little time or energy to do much physical activity. I used to be quite active in sports. But that seems a long time ago now."

"Yes, I understand. Once you get immersed in this University work, the past seems to fade, as if it was lived by another person other than yourself. I felt the same after my first year."

"Do you go to school here?" he quickly followed up, hoping to get a 'yes', in reply.

"Oh, no", she answered, noting he had a kind of diminished affect when she said that. "My classes are conducted on the Ipswich campus. But they don't have all the athletic venues like you have here at St. Lucia.

"What is your major, if you don't mind me asking?"

"Nursing," she replied with some pride in her voice. I start my clinical rotation this coming year. It's my third year toward a Bachelor's Degree in Nursing. After that, I hope to be accepted into their Honours program for my last year. The majority of my clinical time will be at the Royal Brisbane and Women's Hospital, across the river from here."

"Why is that?"

"It's because my major emphasis will be critical care; and the Royal Brisbane receives the majority of these types of patients from around the State."

Soon, however, they had both begun their jogging and the conversation ceased. But arrangements were loosely made that whenever the two of them were on the track at the same time, they would make it a point to speak to each other.

There had developed a major flaw in Colin's earlier life by his not having any brothers or sisters to either associate with or, more importantly, to share with. This prevented him from learning at the most basic level how boys and girls... and ultimately how men and women were supposed to behave towards one another in various situations. In short, easy banter was not something Colin had ever learned how to master. Even his athletic accomplishments and general popularity in school had not allowed him this insight or ability. It all combined to envelope him in a kind of social isolation. And compounding this isolation arose ineptitude and a deep-seated insecurity. Almost immediately, he sensed that maybe this individual, who he had just met, might help him overcome some of this shyness and social awkwardness.

Over that first summer, in between odd jobs for both of them, they began to see more and more of each other. Colin was continually impressed with her independence of spirit and conviction that what she was studying was the right thing for her. He had not yet arrived at the point during his Freshman Year where he felt that same way about studying Economics. Unquestionably, being with her gave him a renewed sense of mission. He, too, would seek to qualify for the Honours program in Economics and out of nowhere he eventually decided that his emphasis would be international economics and finance. Steadily, through his deepening relationship with Jill, he began to expand his horizons, and she had helped him loosen some of the regionalism and parochialism of his youth.

JEFF DAVIS AND BREWSTER COUNTIES TEXAS

EIGHT: FORT DAVIS

Unlike the childhood home locations of Inti and Colin, that of Earnest Blake Corwin, was much different. "E.B.", as he was always called from the moment he left the hospital nursery after his birth on August 12, 1982, was born in Alpine, Texas. His home was to be on a large cattle ranch two or three miles from the small town of Fort Davis, Texas.

For thousands of years the surrounding area had been located along the main trail for one of humanities' most remarkable migrations. The Davis Mountains, which abut Fort Davis, offered nomadic people, passing travelers, settlers, marauders and adventures streams, pastures, shade and protection from the thousands of miles of desert, heat and threat that preceded and followed them. It was like whoever laid out the final geographical landmarks across the Americas decided that whoever had made it this far, after crossing the various deserts to the west and endless prairies to the north, needed this mountainous oasis to renew and redirect their efforts if their destination was further south and east. And so it was for the native Indian tribes of the Mescalero Apaches, Kiowa's and Comanche's.

But inevitably, as the tireless record of evolving civilization shows, in time the will, motivation and skills to settle large sections of land begins to take hold, and it began happening in this prized area in the 1830's. White settlers from the eastern half of the youthful and restless United States were starting to explore and "claim" land in and around the Davis Mountains.

This probably came as no surprise to native peoples of this region. After all, this invasion had been ongoing since the 1600's, as that wave of migration edged across the continent. But these local tribes of west Texas were not the intimidated, somewhat-easily domesticated and reticent ones of the Atlantic and Midwest. The Apaches and Comanche's were unquestionably the most skilled and the fiercest fighting peoples of North America. And it literally took the white settlers building a wall of 29 frontier forts down through central Texas and then extending it westward to the Rio Grande River to protect these newcomers. (see Appendix: **Frontier Forts of Texas**). Manned by the U.S. Army until the Civil War, and then again afterwards, they served as outposts, around which small settlements of civilians began to sprout. Such was the case for Ft. Davis, Texas.

Its frontier fort was constructed in 1854 and was finally decommissioned in 1891. . (see Appendices: **Fort Davis** and **Fort Davis, Texas**) Nestled in the shadow of the Sleeping Lion Mountain, at the southern edge of the Davis Mountains, this natural geological formation provided a barrier and protection for the fort during the Indian Wars. And to this day it stands almost exactly as it was built, perfectly preserved as few others are throughout the country.

That said, this particular fortress provided security for settlers who came west from as far east as Kentucky and Tennessee to begin claiming large swaths of land for their own. And such was the case for the Corwin family. In 1895, settling southeast of the Fort itself, two miles out from what is now Compromise Street, and before the town of Fort Davis was more than a few ship-lap, store fronts, two corner bars, along with the ever-present wooden boardwalks, John and Maud Corwin eventually homesteaded 31 sections of undulating prairie land. Adding to its overall value, three sections of it bordered the eastern edge of Chihuahua Creek. The brown trout and bass... alone... would sometimes provide the family with needed sustenance when other food sources were becoming scarce in the dry months of the year. It was then that the temperature could reach 107 degrees, and the average rainfall of fifteen inches in this area was usually well over.

Ninety-nine percent of Jeff Davis County, of which Ft. Davis is the county seat, is rangeland. Scattered over its hills and mountain sides are a variety of trees and scrubs, including pinion, juniper and oak, along with creosote and yucca. And at 4,900 feet elevation, the area does experience modest amounts of snowfall, and maybe seventy days out of the year there is full cloud cover. Otherwise, region is a blend of high desert, grassland prairie and mountains with an elevation over 8,000 plus feet.

In this setting, it took time to both secure fencing and raise their ranch stock of Herefords and longhorns to the level that John Corwin concluded was the best size for the variability's of the various prairie grasses to sustain them year-round. Eventually, he learned that for each of his one hundred acres, he could add and raise about one and a half calves or cattle. And with 19,200 acres of grazing land, he could safely and profitably manage about 300 head a year. Allowing any more than that and he was asking for losses and weaker stock. And it was this knowledge and heritage that was passed on to the next three generations of family ranchers, which was one day to include Hank and Nelma Corwin, E.B.'s parents.

And Hank and Nelma hoped that E.B. would be the first of a long line of sons to help manage, diversify and grow the ranch, but fate had other plans. Over the next four years, E.B. was to help raise and look after his four younger sisters. And in traditional Texas style, just as giving boys initials for their first-name was a common practice, his parents also decided to add to the first-name merriment by giving his sisters names starting with the same letter... Nin, Nan, Norma and Nattie.   And it became E.B.'s responsibility to watch out for them until such time as they were old enough to begin helping one another. Managing the ranch also required that Nelma help out with multiple chores, other than those associated with routine housekeeping. This meant that E.B., eldest child, had to shoulder much of the earlier years' disciplining and training for his siblings.

It was a role that the boy took on with uncommon dedication and perseverance. But all the while he was developing desires and traits that indicated that his passions in life would not be satisfied simply by staying on the ranch... in any capacity. His dance rhythm, early on, was not like either Inti's or Colin's. His was closer to the jitterbug; being carefree and rootless. He envisioned no pattern or pathway for his life. And being consumed by the care of his four sisters, once he became a teenager, he only wanted to have fun. And the reasonably good income and stability provided by his extended family's past century of ranching on the same piece of land, lent him the opportunity to at least taste such. His parents knew how much he had sacrificed during the first twelve years of his life, so they offered limited objections or reservations to his whims.

Thus began his many days of roaming the countryside on horseback and fishing. However, they had to be intermingled between the mandatory duties all family members had when round-up time began for administering vaccinations, branding, dehorning and castrating. And then there was the late summer and early fall haying to be done. These jobs compressed a rancher's entire year of worry, planning and efforts into less than six months. The open rangeland of the Corwin's Circle "C" Ranch, which was identified on each of their calves with the "©" brand, required the entire family to participate in rounding up their cattle and caring for them. It was their only source of income, aside from whatever part-time jobs Hank, Nelma or E.B. had from time to time. The girls, at this point, were still too young to get paying jobs outside the ranch. But they, no less, had work to do. By the time Nattie, the youngest, was seven, she was cooking the noon meals, while the others were out working in the back-country, barn or corral. These were well-orchestrated activities; they had to be. Dependence on the land requires an intelligence and perseverance that little else can match.

It was a glorious time just the same. Riding the open range, with the surrounding mountains in full view and the valley still groomed in varying shades of yellow, tan and green, was a never-ending source of comfort for E.B. The reds and oranges of the cliffs overlooking Fort Davis gave a perfect backdrop to the undulating prairie.

These were days that demanded skillful and vigorous horseback riding in all directions from the ranch house. Each rider had to swerve, pick out, rope and herd the Circle C's stock to separate them from the other nearby ranches range animals. It was a thrilling time: dusty, fast paced and always accompanied with loud whistling and yelling. And E.B. relished every minute of it.

But it wasn't too long after this initial period of E.B.'s venture into the wider world around him that he had his most telling experience of his adolesence. He got arrested for vandalism and theft. He and a few of his closest friends decided that they wanted to build a small cabin up Limpi Creek, about ten miles northwest of Fort Davis. It was to be a place that they could have rowdy poker games, drink a little bootlegged beer, and maybe even bring a date to just to show her how clever and industrious they all were. It had the appearance of innocence... to all except the land owners and those contractors who lost their building supplies... and to the Jeff Davis County sheriff.

While E.B. had no car to use, four of his friends did, and he joined them after school and on weekend evenings when he had told his parents he was spending time playing baseball at the high school diamond. It was one of the first times he had purposefully lied to them about what he was doing and where he was. And it was the first time he began to be drawn into the world of drink and drugs, because instead of the cabin being used for innocent card games and study hour, it became a center for illicit behavior and drug abuse. E.B. and his friends had discovered ways to pay total strangers to purchase alcohol, and a couple of them had even made the necessary contacts to purchase street drugs. Unlike a few other Texas counties which were still "dry", in other words, no sales of alcohol was allowed; Jeff Davis County was "wet-dry", meaning it sold some but not all varieties of these beverages. But one of the busiest illegal drug highways passed directly through the town of Fort Davis en route to Interstate 10, just north of town, and from there it seeped into almost all America towns and cities. E.B. and his gang of buddies were almost first on the list of buyers for whatever crossed the Mexican border into Texas via the Mexican Chihuahua Desert into Presidio County.

He and his four buddies were ceremoniously arrested in Fort Davis High School one week before his Junior Year ended. They were immediately taken to be booked and briefly placed in the county jail... all but E.B. His fate was different. Despite the objections from Nelma, Hank decided that he was not going to post bond for his son and that he could spend a month inside it to review what all was happening in his life to end up being confined inside a jail.

On the one hand it seemed to have the desired effect, but on the other, it didn't. True enough, following this episode in which E.B. now had a criminal record, he no longer associated with the crowd that urged him into lawless acts. Those days of growing smugness were coming to an end. But at the same time, this decision by Hank left E.B. rootless when he returned to the ranch and his family. He no longer wanted to live or work there. And by now Nan, his second oldest sister, had both shown and declared her intentions to become the next generation's guardian of the ranch. E.B.'s birthright had been superseded by someone who really cared for and worked tirelessly on the ranch.

His senior year in high school passed almost

without notice or comment. His silence at family dinners and holiday gatherings was deafening. His remoteness from everyone, even his mother who he had adored beyond measure, only grew from the day he was released from jail. More and more, he would hitch-hike over to Brewster County and spend time in Alpine, where he was able eventually to pick up a job as a clerk in a hardware store. And before his senior year was finished, he was spending all the week-end nights over there. He never bothered to show up for his high school graduation ceremony.

However, he did raise his overall grade point average enough to be granted admission to Sul Ross State University that next Fall Semester. It was his chance to begin fulltime preparation for leaving the area. That was his one ambition in life now. He no longer felt he had any family and few friends. If he were now on a dance floor, he would simply be standing there... alone, mute and stationary.

NINE: SUL ROSS STATE UNIVERSITY AND BEYOND

With an almost worry-free transition from his high school years into college, E.B. had already established himself in an apartment off the Alpine's main street and was enrolled in the Natural Resources Management's Conservation Biology program that first day of the 2000 Fall Enrollment. He was transformed by this newly acquired independence, both physically and financially. His work and some tuition assistance through the University's endowment program gave him full confidence that he would be able to pay his way through college.

Only his oldest sister, Nin, kept in close contact with him. This being her senior year in Fort Davis High School, she was able to convince their parents to let her have her own car. And she drove over to Sul Ross each weekend that Fall. Theirs was a relationship that he treasured; it was the only one with his family that was judgment-free. They shared private thoughts and aspirations with each other, knowing that no one outside their immediate confidences would ever know what they were.

And surprising, even to her, was E.B.'s long

anticipated return to dating. After his incarceration one and a half years earlier, he had few, if any, dates with any of the local girls. But when he began working the summers in Alpine, he did have a few double and triple dates with other couples. At that, there was nothing serious or long-term. But his Freshman Year was different. He became involved with a wonderful freshman who came from Houston and was enrolled in the Animal Science Preventive Veterinary Program. It would have been easier and closer for her to have studied at Texas A&M's School of Veterinary Medicine, but her health had been affected by living in the high humidity of the Gulf Coastal area. She had developed moderately severe asthma as a result. Coming out to Alpine suited her and her family, as well as greatly improving her asthmatic condition; and she could take the prerequisite courses for admission into A&M's program in two years. It was all just a matter of taking the right courses and achieving at least a "B" grade in each.

They met at the Freshman Picnic, a traditional gathering sponsored by the University for each Incoming Class just prior to their first week of classes. It is held in the Commons area, in the center of the campus. And their Freshman Class had 380 students, which was a little smaller than usual. It was a lovely September evening, with temperatures in the low 70's by 6:30 p.m. when the bar-be-cue ribs, potato salad, baked beans, ice tea and Texas toast was about to be served. Long tables and accompanying benches had been set out for everyone to use. A slight breeze was stirring, which gave rise to just a hint of juniper in the air, after a late afternoon shower passed through.

E.B. was late arriving, having to close the hardware store on Main Street, where he had worked all summer as a clerk and stocker. He rushed into the midst of students who were now well into being served and seating themselves. Somewhat frantically, he finally was able to get a plate of food and his drink and then looked around for an empty seat. All the way over on one side he did see what looked like a space at the edge of one table. And when he got there he couldn't help but notice the person sitting across from him. He learned later that her name was Joan.

She radiated warmth and a spirit of good will, as she greeted him with, "We were about to think you'd never show up!" It made him laugh and put him immediately at ease. And from that exchange, their conversation was nonstop for the remainder of the meal and into the evening. It was something he never imagined would happen to him: to meet someone so nice, so open, and so lovely... all immediately upon the first contact he made at the school.

Of note, she did confide to him the reasons that she was going to study Pre-Veterinary Medicine. To begin with, it was because she had always been an avid horseback rider and caretaker for her own horse since she could remember. She grew up on a small farm outside Houston. And it was when she and E.B. got up from the table that first night that he noticed that she had a rather marked limp when stepping on her right leg. As it turned out, she told him that as a young girl, on one of the first times she was allowed to ride a horse independently, her uncle had not cinched the saddle on tight enough, and when she was at a gallop and needed to turn to avoid hitting a telephone post, the saddle slipped and she struck her head against the pole. That injury caused extensive brain damage at the time, but by the time she and E.B. met, all that remained was a noticeable limp. She had to wear a short-leg brace due to residual weakness of that lower leg.   And if anything, her telling him this made this first contact more memorable.

Most surprising of all was that they had most of their Freshman Classes in common that first year. She also had to take English composition/technical writing, U.S. History, Calculus I and II, General Chemistry and Biology with E.B. The two of them were to become inseparable. And it is safe to say that for E.B., it was the first time he had fallen in love with someone outside his immediate family. Joan brought a joy and comfort to him that he had never known before. They shared all their thoughts and feelings, besides the usual collegiate banter and discourse about their classes and homework. It was a productive and creative relationship, in addition to a loving one. And one that flourished through that first year and the next summer. It was a routine that was never fully recaptured in E.B.'s life thereafter; the comfort, peace and pleasure of her company and the surroundings gave him precious memories for the years to come.

Ahead for both of them were more classes that would begin to emphasize their particular majors. For E.B. they would include classes in soils, forest and fire ecology, range inventory and analysis, mammalogy, ornithology and herpetology. For Joan they would entail her taking classes in the Animal Science program on campus. Their futures looked bright and promising. And the world around them was at peace.

Until the beginning of that Fall Semester of 2001, and then everything changed for him after that September attack in New York City. An anger arose inside him that he'd never experienced before. It was like somehow he had personally allowed this to happen. All his life, it seemed, he had been protecting someone or something... first his sisters, then the ranch's horses and livestock, then after his being in jail, his own sense of self and trying to insure his own right to make a mistake but still prove his worth, and just recently… Joan. But surrounding all this was his deep affection for the land and this country. He'd never had to put it into words or explain it to anyone; it was just a part of him: the beauty of the surrounding mountains and valleys, the streams, the breezes in the evening. It was this precious land and her people. And now, without any warning, something so cruel and senseless had been committed on innocents. He knew he had to protect others. It was who he was.

Knowing that he had to discuss all this with someone, he did a few days later with both Joan and Nin. Neither were overly concerned by his remarks; everyone was extremely upset and fighting mad at what had happened. And yet there was a certain unnerving intensity about his feelings, and they seemed to leave open the possibility that he may act on them in some surprising manner. It was Joan he told first.

"I'm going to join the Army!" he announced to her one evening after they were walking back into town.

"You what"!!" she replied.

"I have to do something. I'm not comfortable just trying to go on with my schooling right now. And as much as I want to be right here with you, this is something I have to do."

"But your studies, your dreams, our dreams and the plans we have talked about so often and so passionately. What about them? Us?" And then she began to sob.

He couldn't bring himself to say anything for a while after that. Her crying and the heartfelt expression of how she joined her life's dreams with his was not a surprise in any way, but the depth of her reaction to his decision confused him. Never before had anyone expressed such deep commitment to his being in their life. He was about to cause someone great pain, and it made him feel nauseated... very like he was about to vomit. It was the most intense series of feelings he had ever known. His living mattered deeply to someone. In response, he simply turned to her and gathered her into his arms, and they both quietly began to weep.

Eventually, he tipped her head up and looked into her eyes and said, with all the commitment and determination that could possibly be residing in a nineteen year old country boy from the empty spaces of West Texas, "I will always be there for you. Finish your studies, become the veterinarian you so want to be, I'll keep constantly in touch with you, and then we can be together once you've finished your studies and training."

"Do you promise?" she asked in a voice and a manner that stayed with him the rest of his life.

"With as sincere and humble a commitment as it is possible to make." Then taking off his high school graduation ring, he gently slipped it onto her left hand ring finger. "Please take this. My ring will always be yours to keep, and my love for you will never lessen. Know this, dear Joan: you are the most important person in the world to me. That will never change."

They talked far into the night after this. It was a crossroads that neither ever forgot, and only time and events far beyond their control would foretell if the both of them would be able to keep their vows of commitment. The world had begun a momentous upheaval. Reason, sound judgment, the simplest gestures of humanity and tolerance were being replaced with the darkest side of humanity's covetous and ravenous will to take and to kill.

The cycle was beginning anew, and no one… anywhere… knew how this was going to end. The melodies were fading, the dance floor was emptying. The growling sounds of revenge and retribution were replacing the often muted sounds of music and joy. Once again, the world was being drug into war.

And two days later E.B. was able to hitch a ride from Alpine to Marfa, and once there, to catch a bus leaving north to El Paso. At his destination, he was planning to see an Army recruiter and to enlist.

THE DIVERGENCE

PARIS

TEN: THE WEST BANK AND RADICALIZATION

The next segment of Inti, Colin and E.B.'s individual journeys becomes more defining as to what or who accompanies them in their establishing a lifetime pattern of decisions and actions and whether any of these entails dancing, and what might be the accompaniment to their particular dance. And if there is, will there be any rhythm and consistent pattern to these dance steps or will they be random movements, resulting in disjointed jerking and flailing about? Will there be proper timing or pauses for emphasis or reflection by the dancer, or will it simply be chaotic and disjointed? Or will there be any accompanying music? Will it incorporate harmonies, something with a melody or will it simply contain discordant notes, like scraping sounds, creating a raw, alarming noise?

Will they choose a partner, if dancing should eventually become possible? Or will there be many partners? Will they share the dance with them, being generous and gracious, allowing that partner the opportunity to display their own talents and skills? And will they eventually choose to settle with one partner? Or will they be too distracted, self-possessed, abusive, dominating... and selfish to do so?

And finally when does dancing of any kind, for any of them, become out of reach or impossible? Each of them has begun their lives with a particular dance. Childhood provides that as one of its gifts. It's there for each of us to practice and expand upon. Whether we choose to do so is an entirely different matter, as our three characters are about to see. Will they become too rich, too powerful, too smug, too isolated or just too stupid to follow a course that grants them this ongoing gift? It's a question that lies in wait for each of us as we make those seemingly random and unimportant decisions each day. But as they accumulate, the outcome will certainly determine if there is to be music, poise, grace and dancing in each of our lives. And now it's time to find out whether that is possible for these three individuals.

Inti, of course, did fly to Paris from La Paz, but not with the intention of simply interviewing and then returning to La Paz; traveling with him were his laptop and an oversized suitcase. Arriving sometime later within the next month via ship were two trunks, filled with books, research papers and an unfinished thesis, along with the rest of his clothing and the few mementoes he possessed. He had arranged with the shipper that he would be notifying their Paris office of his local address ahead of the trunks' arrival.

Landing at the Orly Airport from Lima, Peru, where Inti's second leg of the trip from Las Paz transported him, was at 8:15 p.m. on August 15, 2007. There had been a brief stopover in Amsterdam beforehand. He was anxious to begin the third and last year of laboratory work and thesis preparation toward receiving his PhD. He hoped to become fully examined and his thesis approved by the end of 2008. Knowing only that he was to be admitted into Sorbonne University, when he hailed a taxi to take him into the City proper, he could only tell the driver this much as far as a destination. And by way of an introduction to his now having to speak French, the language he so wanted to master from his earliest University days, he asked the cab driver if he could suggest somewhere in that vicinity for him to stay at least for that night.

Pleased that his last fare for the night could speak French, the driver immediately replied, "Certainly, sir," in the rapid-paced manner so characteristic of most large metropolitan areas of the world, and certainly as Inti would find years later, so different from the much slower, undulating cadence of those Frenchmen in the midlands and southern France. "I know of a perfect place in the Latin Quarter, just a block or two from the University. I know the proprietor well, and in fact I, too, live not too far from there with my family. Do you plan to stay in Paris long?"

Pleased that he understood everything told him, Inti replied, "Oh yes. Once I am finished with my studies and thesis, I hope to live here permanently."

"Where are you coming from?" the driver quickly inquired.

"From La Paz, Bolivia."

"I'm not even sure where that is."

"Believe me," Inti quickly interjected, "it's a long, long way from here." I went to University there. I'm actually from the Yungas, which is the mountainous interior, northeast of La Paz. It's where the coffee you drink every morning comes from."

At that, the cab driver laughed and seemed to wordlessly indicate that it was time for him to concentrate on the mounting flow of traffic into the City for the eight miles it took to get to the Peripherique, the expressway bordering the southern portion of Paris. So pleased that he was nearly there, Inti just settled back in the seat and watched the flow of traffic and a gradual build-up of larger and denser buildings come into view. And as soon as they turned onto the artery that led to the Blvd. St. Michel, he was able to see the upper portion of the Eiffel Tower, certainly the tallest, most identifiable landmark in the city. Upon seeing it, he knew his lifelong plan was at last coming true. This was no dream.

Twisting through narrow side streets and alongside crowded sidewalks, he saw people just finishing their dinner or sipping coffee and engaged in the other national past time: conversation. A few blocks before they reached their destination, the driver said he was turning onto Rue Saint-Jacques and soon he would be passing the original Sorbonne University, which was now called the University of Paris. And that his final destination would be just a block or two beyond it on the right hand side of the street. Slowing down, the driver eventually pulled to a stop in front of an older building, sandwiched between others which looked quite similar. Each one had a small, ornate entrance doorway, with multiple small balconies extending six stories, to their top floor. Each balcony had cast iron railings jutting out in a small semicircle around it. The particular building he was directed to enter by the driver appeared to have maybe five or six apartments at each of these levels. It looked quite old, but tidy and well groomed.

Thanking the driver and paying him with some of the French Francs that he had recently converted at the airport exchange kiosk from the Bolivian currency he had brought with him, he eagerly pulled his suitcase and on-board carrying case, which contained his laptop, out from the back seat and waved the driver off.

After explaining his circumstances for coming to Paris; that he was not a tourist and that the taxi driver had recommended this hotel, plus that his driver knew the owner, the concierge made a quick telephone call and then said that the owners would be glad to offer him lodging on a month-to-month basis at a reasonable rate in one of their smaller apartments on the top floor. It seemed too good to be true, and Inti quickly accepted. But it did require that he walk the six flights of stairs any time he went down or came up to the apartment. There were no elevators when this building was constructed, and none were ever installed. Once he managed to maneuver his large, oversized suitcase up the twisting stairwell, he set it down and immediately went over to the street-side window and looked out. There before him lay the most spectacular sight of his life: the sprawling inner city of Paris. For once in his life, he felt like he was home at last.

His apartment was a single room, which contained both a toilet and a side-by-side bidet. They were fully exposed against the outside wall, with a window on either side, from which he could lean forward and look down onto the street below. And fortunately, there were both a bed and a dresser included in the rent as well. It being 11 p.m. by the time he got settled, he quickly unpacked a few essentials from his suitcase; but before he used any, he collapsed on top of the bed. The thirty-three hour flight had been exhausting, and he fell quickly sound asleep.

Tomorrow would be soon enough to shave, shower and begin exploring where his classes and laboratories were located.

Almost immediately, upon his setting out the next morning to find a nearby café to have some coffee and a croissant, he was struck by the uniqueness of the Latin Quarter, with all its quaint shops, cafes, bustling sidewalks and historical surroundings. Flowers were bunched or planted everywhere, and their colors highlighted the muted gray, blue and black native stone and brick buildings and sidewalks. Alive and colorful were blended perfectly with the old and stately. It was truly enchanting. And it was the Paris that he had always dreamt about.

But before he began to take in too much of the scenery following his light breakfast, he wanted to orient himself as to where he was to work and to study. So, with his Letter of Acceptance in hand he began a survey of a five or six square block area. (see Appendix: **Map of Paris**) And eventually he ended up on Boulevard Saint Germain and within another six blocks he stopped at the intersection of Pont de Sully Bridge and Quai Saint-Bernard. It was there, at the junction of the Latin Quarter and Jussieu that he came face-to-face with what were to become the most significant influences in his life from that moment on. The first was on the southeast corner of this intersection; it was the Institut du Monde Arabe and the other was the UPMC (Sorbonne Universities) or more specifically the Universite Pierre et Marie Curie... the soon-to-be center for his nuclear physics study and work. Further adding to his excitement of discovery was that Le Mosquee was about a half mile walk from the University. This was to be the worship center that he would come to for daily prayers and various meetings which ultimately changed the course of history.

It was an absolute miracle; something he felt was directly related to his recent conversion to Islam. He knew it was a sign. He felt chosen to do some great deed for Allah and for his faith. It was a to be a true blessing to have these most vital institutions within a short distance from his new home. He could now concentrate on his studies and thesis without worrying about travel and transportation.

Over the course of the next year, there were continuing life-altering changes and opportunities that occurred or presented themselves to Inti. And it must be said at this juncture that while Inti, or any other individual, who is caught up in his or her maneuvering through the formative stages of a career, finishing years of an extended education or completing mastery of advanced skills that there is another ongoing process just as intensely taking place. It involves the evolving psychological dimensions of one's character and our responses to challenges, new ideas and once-familiar customs. Some of the resulting changes are, to some extent, what one is predisposed to develop through inherent, genetic markings; but others are the result of societal or cultural influences. And most are driven by the decisions, consciously and unconsciously made by each of us.

Their manifestation can take the form of obvious, outward-appearing changes; which in Inti's case, after his first year living in Paris, was that he began sporting a moustache. One might say that this can be a decision anyone can make simply by conforming to trends that exist in the general society, i.e. every man of a certain age has one. Or it can be related to the dance routines that evolve in each of our lives; it could signal the need or desire to project a certain image. And so it was for Inti. He no longer intended to let the waltz be his dance of choice. He was gradually leaning toward another style of dance. It was prompted by two more landmarks in his journey.

The first was that in that next year he did distinguish himself at UPMC with his thesis on nuclear fissionable materials and a new and significantly easier process to enhance and modify them. So earth-shaking were his conclusions that the French Atomic Energy Commission (CEA) and the French Nuclear Safety Authority (ASN) immediately placed a "TOP SECRET" stamp on it and required that it not be read or even discussed outside an approved military jurisdiction. Further, all his mentors and any professors who assisted or discussed this thesis were sworn to complete secrecy about its contents. The simplicity and uniqueness of his seminal work was to alter entirely the level of threat imposed by any country presently having or producing radioactive materials for any purpose. If the atomic age genie had partially emerged out of the magical lamp before, he was now standing alongside it, with hands on hips, waiting for his master's command. The little brown-skinned man from the Yungas had transformed the thinking and threat level previously possessed within the scientific world.

The second landmark was that in that same year he began to regularly attend and observe the five prayers of worship; and whenever possible, to do so at The Mosque located some distance behind the University. In addition, he also attended classes and conferences at the Arab Center and at The Mosque. It was at one of these classes that he became friends with the Malik family, who had emigrated from Algeria in 1960, two years before the Algerian War ended. They, too, lived in the Latin Quarter, and they welcomed Inti into their family with warmth and the customary Islamic hospitality. And it was at one of these gatherings that a cousin of theirs came to an extended family feast after Ramadan.

She was in the final year of a medical school Residency Program at the Hospital du Val-de-Grace about one mile from Inti's residence. Little could anyone have imaged that a few years later her caring for many of France's Government Ministers in this hospital, and the social connection this later provided Inti, would have so horrifying an outcome.

Her name was Froncett. Her piercing black eyes and long, perfectly combed and styled black hair, along with the traditional Algerian dress riveted Inti at that first introduction. Fortunately for him, the same person who had such poor success with meeting and establishing any lasting relationship with a girl or woman before, he was able to impress her with his quiet manner and singular intelligence. And within the next year he asked her father for permission to marry her. Both he and she agreed, and the wedding that followed was by all accounts spectacular.

He was now ready to advance to the next dance level: a dance partner had been chosen. But that was to be the easiest step. The remaining dance steps are never easy, unless of course one or both of the partners is uninterested in beginning to refine and perfect what they've initiated. In that case, the music and dancing soon stops, and for some it never resumes again.

Upon his receiving his PhD, Inti was immediately approached with an offer so generous and open-ended from the French Atomic Energy Commission, which was speaking in behalf of the military heads of the Force de Frappe, the branch of the French Armed Services dedicated solely to the upkeep, management and improvement of their nuclear weapons, that he could only nod "yes" to their offer. Soon thereafter he was assigned to work in the military section of the Atomic Commission at their facility in Valduc, about 160 miles southeast of Paris and 27 miles northeast of Dijon. No one could have guessed the horror that would result from this invitation and its eager acceptance.

That was because in the year that Inti was at the University, his strict fidelity and adherence to the tenets of Islam became progressively more evident to the Iman and to certain others in the mosque and in the Institute. And as this intense observance progressed, his every move was monitored carefully and thoroughly. It was only a matter of time before he was approached by a representative of a highly covert cell of individuals... unless of course Inti decided to approach one of them first.

In the meantime, there was a progression of family duties and responsibilities that diverted Inti's focus to some degree. And that was primarily due to his finally experiencing the age-old tradition of establishing his bona fides of manhood. As conflicted and shunned as he was in college and graduate school in La Paz, once he established himself in Paris and he and Froncett became mutual admirers, glimpses of his former cultural imperatives or ancestral rituals began to surface. And this primarily took on the role of his aspiring to become an impregnator.

Leading up to this climactic role, he began to display signs of machismo by exerting increasingly more control of what Froncett did and how she dressed and behaved. To her surprise, he expressed a strong desire for them to have many children, and she noticed that he seemed almost preoccupied with outwardly expressing so-called manly ambitions and goals.

This behavior was not especially new for her to see take place; after all, she was born and raised in one or more of the countries bordering the Mediterranean Sea. She had seen the same type of behavior displayed in her father and with her brothers as they inched their way into what they proudly described as "manhood". It just seemed a bit overblown with Inti; almost like it was an act he felt he needed to play. But even with her being a licensed physician, the mores and customs of her heritage allowed this metamorphosis to proceed without comment. Ultimately, however, she did feel loved and cared for, as did their children. And by the time Inti became fully involved with what he later described as an offshoot of the Muslim Brotherhood, he and Froncett had two sons.

In all likelihood, the cell's using this title was a cover for something more sinister. But using it would disguise their activities and prevent the French Secret Service from monitoring their every move. The Brotherhood had achieved worldwide recognition as a relatively peaceful organization, with some glaring exceptions, such as those members who were implicated in the murder of Anwar Sadat of Egypt. And yet in other countries bordering North Africa and the Arabian Peninsula, their presence was not a source of major concern to their leaders and those elsewhere. And the French authorities decided it was better to tolerate an organization that didn't overtly subscribe to violence or to an uncompromising view of non-Muslims than to ban them altogether.

What ultimately led Inti to accept an invitation to meet with the members of this select group, carefully and painstakeningly burrowed deep in the substrate of the largest of the social and political organizations at The Mosque in Paris was a seething anger, which first appeared in his college years in La Paz. It was born out of the suffering and poverty that he witnessed his parents and family endure, and from the bitterness he later experienced at being rejected so often by the upper crust of La Paz and the University. His being shunned and treated like he was third or fourth best ignited a desire to get even, to show others that he was no one to ignore or demean. And over time, as the members of this select group of Islamists watched and waited, they saw that their opportunity to recruit and radicalize Inti had arrived. But only the most highly educated amongst them approached and groomed him. They knew it would take some time to gain his complete trust and willingness to undertake the plan they had been hatching since he first appeared at their prayers, and they learned of his studies and thesis. They sensed that here… at last… was someone gifted enough and with enough animosity toward all infidels to undertake the most significant event of the twenty-first century.

That first meeting with Inti required further monitoring of his normal work week's schedule. It had to be seamlessly woven into his normal pattern of activities once he was off work. During his four-day work week, Inti was housed at the Valduc facility but as soon as his week was done, he drove immediately back to Paris on Highway A-5. And after a night and day with his family, it was common for him to spend the majority of his other time at the mosque in prayer and in meetings. Froncett was consumed with her job at the hospital as lead nurse in the General Surgery section. They had hired a governess to help with household chores and managing their children. It was not as important to Inti to be with them as it was to just say he had them. Having many children again served to bolster his sense of manhood, as it did with those he associated with at the mosque.

It was at the end of 2011 that The Plan was finally agreed upon by the clandestine group that called themselves al Haboob. (see Appendix: **al Haboob**) At that point, they knew it would take a full year to fully develop and implement. The urgency of timing was now critical. Inti had to be incorporated into The Plan immediately.

ELEVEN: LONDON

While Colin's trademark dance in his younger years was more like the Tango, mixed occasionally with the jitterbug, University discipline and challenges markedly lessened the exuberance of those dance rhythms. There still was some background music in his life as he matriculated through the sophomore, junior and honour program years of his studies. And he would freely admit it was all due to the presence of Jill in his life. Equally evident were the telltale signs of him establishing a rudimentary pattern of seeking to enter the coveted circle of manhood through the role as a provider. And it began with his return to sports, while much less in team-centered competition; but still even more intensely as an individual enthusiast and sometimes spectator. His running with Jill, taking up tennis and golf were examples of this. In addition, during these years, particularly the last two as he finished work on his Masters in International Finance and Economics, he solidified his deepening sense of an absolute self-reliance. This personal quest was not at the exclusion of Jill, but it was to him like building a bulwark against insecurity and isolation, his two childhood and early college-years' nemeses.

The importance of Jill in his life could not be overstated. She centered his aspirations and motivations. And while she was a year ahead of him in her careerstudies and training, he used this as a source of further motivation to complete his Masters Degree. Supplementing his studies, his academic advisor suggested he try securing an internship of some sort with a bank in Brisbane that had international ties. He felt it would serve as a stepping stone and maybe even an avenue into some fulltime employment once he finished his University studies. His professor suggested he approach the one international bank that he knew of for such a position. It was located in downtown Brisbane.

Realizing that this was most likely the surest way to insure employment in the area of his educational emphasis, Colin immediately followed up on this suggestion and made an appointment with the bank's Personnel Department. It was located on Queen Street, one block from Anzac Square in one direction and one block from the Brisbane River. It was in the center of the city.

And to his good fortune, he was able to secure a position, once the interviewers saw his course work, grades and recommendations from his professors. By his getting this internship, it meant that he could finally quit his tutoring and teaching undergraduates for income. The internship would pay for all his registration fees, housing and incidentals. He could focus entirely on finishing the Masters Degree, all the while getting practical experience in international finance and banking. Out of this experience, he anticipated that a focus for his work life would emerge. And it did.

Once he finished his internship, he was offered fulltime employment in their Brisbane office. And equally important, his supervisor was going to let him pursue his passion that had become so evident over the last two years: improving the quality of everyday life for the poor in communities throughout Asia through increasing their access to the most basic financial services. And one of the mediums that he would use would be his love of sports and incorporating the development of sports venues at the same time in these communities. And this he did with great passion over the next three years, traveling throughout the region and establishing a highly visible resume as he did.

Once Jill graduated from her Master's Program in Nursing, their prearranged plan to marry was finalized. Colin still had another year in his Masters Program, but he was established well enough at the bank and at the University that neither of them anticipated that marrying at this time would cause any undue hardship. And because Jill's parents and siblings lived in or around Nambour, Queensland, that was where the ceremony took place; in the local park just outside the center of downtown. A railroad embankment and trestle hid flow of city traffic in and out of town from peering at most of their ceremony. It was held on a bright December 12th day.

The weather was perfect. The ceremony was to begin at 5 p.m., to be followed by a reception that was to be held in the same area. Minimal decorating was necessary, given the natural beauty surrounding them. Towering over them were four magnificent macadamia trees, bursting with ripening nuts that were just beginning to fall. And to one side was a natural barrier of red, pink and purple poinsettias and bougainvilleas and at the podium were bouquets of native yellow banksias, waddle and wax flower; their yellow, white and violet colors provided a rainbow-like atmosphere that was gloriously bright and gay. To Colin and his parents, it matched his bride's personality perfectly. The ceremony, dinner, music and dancing that followed lasted almost until dawn. Nothing could have been more perfect.

And over the next two years, while Jill worked at the same hospital where she did the majority of her training, she gave birth to two children, the last of which had a moderately severe endocrine deficiency and this resulted in some minor retardation, along with a marked loss of mobility. He was a special needs child, but as time went on, both Sarah, his older sister, and each of his parents knew he was a gift instead of a burden. And for Colin, in particular, Zackary, or "Zackers" as everyone called him, became the lodestone in his quest for manhood as a provider in those first years of their marriage.

It was during his third year at the Brisbane bank that he was offered his first promotion, but it would entail him and his family moving to London. Building on his work with undeveloped countries of Asia, the London headquarters was so impressed that they wanted him to extend that same type of work, coupled with creating loan packages for both communities and governments in Africa and South America. And it would not involve as much travel. But with the main office in London communicating almost daily with their 7,500 branch offices overseas in 87 countries, it was clear he would be extremely busy. The position would entail mostly coordinating with branches in the countries identified with special needs and which offered a sound basis to extend loans. All the while, he needed to make the equally critical follow-up for both determining and insuring success. Both Jill and Colin were thrilled at the opportunity, and he accepted the position after his first and only trip back to London.

So at the unheard of age of 27, he and his family bid their Queensland families farewell and flew from Brisbane to London on January 9, 2009, leaving summer behind and heading into their first-ever, actual winter season. Upon arrival, after staying briefly in a hotel in the suburb of Richmond, they needed to find a permanent location to move into and, equally important, a place for their household goods which were coming by ship in another month. And following the recommendation of his Vice-President of the Department of Overseas Development, they found a lovely cottage for sale in Kew. (see Appendix: **Kew Village**).

It was not a random suggestion of his Vice-President. Many employees of the London bank had moved there over the course of their employment. The area was located at the apex of a bend in the Thames River, west of London. The town was first settled in the year 1327 because of its evolving advantages of having multiple transportation links. Initially, all travel was via the river itself, but after a bridge was eventually built over it multiple forms of travel eventually became possible, whether by foot, horseback, train, subway, auto or the "underground". But for Colin, his primary mode of commuting was to take the subway train to Richmond and then transfer on to central London.

Their two-story, Tudor Revival home was over one hundred years old. (see Appendix: **Colin and Jill Tudor Revival Home**) It was instantaneous choice for the family once they saw the outside of it, and then everything was confirmed when they entered each room inside. It was perfect. The exposed beams scattered throughout the home gave it warmth, even without any wood or gas stoves lit or turned on. And even the pervasive London fog this time of year couldn't detract from the innate comfort of their new home.

And once their furniture arrived and was in place, the Kennard household was intact again and their spirits were buoyant. Even little Zackers seemed to sense the relief and calm that deepened with each passing day. Any reservations about moving all this distance were soon resolved.

But there was one variation from the life they were used to living back in Brisbane. While there, Jill still worked up to thirty hours a week; but before they left for London, she suggested to Colin that she not work for a year or so to focus on getting Zackary further along in his rehabilitation by practicing his physiotherapy drills more diligently. And she knew that Sarah would need extra attention being in a strange environment and yet not quite ready to start any preschool program.

In the meantime, Colin had to begin his new job with zeal and unparalleled determination. He was by far the youngest person in the department, and unknown to him there was a large office pool started even before his arrival. It involved wagering how long he would last at the firm. The majority of picks were that he'd be gone in less than three months. Some even bet that he'd be gone in less than a month. The primary reason for the latent hostility was because he was an outsider... someone from Australia: a onetime British colony. The vast majority of the wagers were staff members of his highly prestigious department; one which was focused on by the press and other media most often. This was due to the ongoing human interest stories it spawned and their often stunning initial results in helping under-developed communities and countries gain an economic foothold on stability and genuine entrepreneurship. Most of those betting had been schooled at Exeter and then went on to Oxford or Cambridge. They were at the top of the creamy layer of a still, mostly stratified English society. Colin, to them, was a colonial; nothing more.

And at this time, it needs to be noted that in the course of human history, the single most defining choice each young male must make is whether he will take the ritualistic path into manhood or take the less visible and much less touted one into becoming a man. There is a multitude of side trails, pitfalls and potential delays associated with either choice, but the latter is by far the loneliest and most challenging.

In the case of achieving ritualized manhood, many cultures, both ancient and current, started this process with their adolescent... even preadolescent boys. This occurs by their being circumcised or sent off into a vast ocean or the bush or the wilds to forage for themselves. Afterwards, they are expected to both survive and/or bring back some large or ferocious animal or its hide. And other cultures expect that this highly sought-after recognition for acceptance into a given society's cult of manhood will begin at a predetermined age beyond that of a youth. It could be at the time he attains his first full-time job, enters the military, graduates from a distant educational institution or simply moves away from his traditional childhood home for the first time. These manhood rituals can easily become complex and taxing... both to the aspiring individual and to those around him. They can even become deadly.

And as mentioned before, Colin had, to some extent, begun his manhood quest in his youth, particularly with his initial success with various sporting events and later with some scholastic success during his University years. But the most notable change that Jill noticed, and one she eventually had to challenge, was the one that began at a most precarious and potentially deadly time: when an individual male enters his twentieth decade or early-to-mid thirties. But it probably should be noted that this pivotal change could be delayed to the fourth or fifth decade of a self-seeking, male's lifetime. But more specifically in Colin's case, he had been working in London for two years and was then 29 years old, the same age as Inti when he became involved in the more sinister elements of the Muslim Brotherhood.

Colin's provider image of manhood took on three more pronounced affectations. He was becoming obsessed with having the proper image, even when he was at home. He had to dress a certain way and speak with a certain accent. And even with Jill's remarkable Australian talent of ferreting out fakery and bombast, he persisted. Further, she observed that he would stand up to her whenever she would challenge him or if there were innocent slights or insults of a minor nature. He was becoming fixated on attaining and then maintaining a certain image... however awkward and painful it might appear to others. And finally, and the most serious to her, was that he appeared to be taking unnecessary risks both at work, when he was driving and even quite possibly with other female employees.

It was at an after-dinner discussion that they were having that this all came to a crisis point.

"Colin, I need to talk to you," Jill began.

"I'm afraid I just don't have time," he replied. "Today's schedule was brutal, and I've got to get some rest before I leave tomorrow on that flight to Nigeria."

"I wouldn't be so sure of that," she countered.

"What do you mean?" he spun around from his closet, as he was deciding what clothes to pack for the one week journey, to be accompanied by his office associate, Darlene.

"You left your cell phone on while you were in the bathroom. It was lying on the bedside table, and you forgot to put it on mute or record. It was easy for me to hear whatever the caller was saying."

"So?"

"So it was Darlene."

At that, his mood and bombast lessened quite noticeably.

"What did she have to say?" he asked, his voice lowering with each word.

"The usual one might expect for someone traveling to a far off place, with one major exception. She said, and I will quote it for you: 'I am busy packing what I will be wearing on the plane. I will be arriving at the airport at 6 a.m. tomorrow.' And then she signed off with: 'I am so excited about our being able to spend this time together, darling. All my love.'

The silence that followed was the most painful of either of their lives.

Then Jill spoke again.

"NOW! THIS IS WHAT YOU ARE GOING TO DO! YOU WILL CALL HER BACK NOW, WITH ME STANDING HERE; AND YOU WILL CANCEL THESE FLIGHT PLANS!

"YOU WILL THEN CALL YOUR BOSS AND TELL HIM THAT YOU ARE NOT FLYING TO NIGERIA OR ANYWHERE ELSE FOR THE NEXT YEAR!

"I DON'T CARE WHAT REASON OR EXCUSE

YOU USE, JUST DO IT!

"Then you will begin a process of getting some control of your life and finding a place for us in yours. Otherwise, quicker than you ever saw events and disaster befall you, this career of yours and our marriage will dissolve before your eyes. DO YOU HEAR ME?!! DO YOU UNDERSTAND WHAT I AM SAYING?!!"

And so it was. For the next year there were no excursions outside London by Colin, and he did arrange to have another office assistant take Darlene's place, after she was promoted to another position. And as bright as his future looked at the bank, during this year his reduced visibility and ritualistic bombast did lower his standing with upper management. But at the same time, he did regain some of Jill's trust and began a return to a more meaningful and authentic role as provider for his family. And to prove his fidelity and love, he scheduled a week's vacation for them, their first since coming to London, for a week's stay in Paris in December. They'd be there for the Christmas holiday.

TWELVE: FRANKFURT, GERMANY

E.B. had to wait three hours in Marfa for the bus that travels between Laredo and El Paso. It was midnight when he finally arrived in El Paso's Central Transit Center; and of course the streets were basically empty, except for those who were bedding down in alleyways or in corners of stores and office buildings. Homeless people in El Paso were a growing threat to the health and safety of those working downtown, and a large shelter for them was being constructed at the time E.B. arrived.

Because of the on-the-spurt-of-the-moment decision he made to enlist, he had made no other arrangements for lodging. He hadn't even told his family that he was doing this. He knew they would probably be upset, but this was a decision that he needed little consultation to make. It was only Joan that he wanted to tell in hopes of getting her approval. And as far as their future plans, he had no idea what might be possible. But he did want to fulfill his promise of fidelity to her... if it was at all possible. But being nineteen years old and volunteering for military service were not the best predictors of follow-through with such an oath.

And as is the case in most large cities, somewhere

close by a bus terminal there usually is a hotel which is open all night. E.B. asked his driver if there might be, and he was directed to one that was two blocks away. It was a sleepless night, but he was glad to at least be off the streets. This was the first time he had ever been in a city, much less one the size of El Paso.

He was so nervous the next morning that he had no desire to eat breakfast. He found a map in the city's telephone directory, where he was able to see that the street where the Army Recruiter was located was about ten blocks from where he was. Using his hotel room telephone, the Army Recruiter's answering machine indicated that their office would be open by the time he walked there. His nervousness mounted steadily as he made his way in that direction. He had no idea what he would say or what he wanted to do if and when he was asked what specialty or training he preferred. It was only when he got to the store front window and saw the picture of a helicopter flying above a group of soldiers looking up at it that he knew that was what he'd like to do: fly one of those.

The recruiter had only arrived a few minutes before E.B. walked in the door. He was immediately impressed with his size and fit-appearing physique. By this time E.B. was easily six feet two inches tall and weighed at least 190 pounds. His years on the ranch had endowed him with a muscular build, and the recruiter knew if this newcomer was seeking to enlist, he would have no problem filling his weekly recruitment quota.

"Can I help you?" the neatly dressed staff sergeant asked. And immediately he could see that even without weighing this individual, he would meet the 211 pound upper limit for his height.

"Yes, sir," E.B. replied, realizing right away his voice was too loud for the small office. Lowering his voice an octave, he added, "I would like to join the Army if it is possible."

"When did you plan on doing that?"

"Today... right now, if I could," he added as he walked steadily forward to the recruiter's desk.

"How old are you then?"

"I'm nineteen, Sir. I was just starting my second year in college, but then all this happened back East, and I knew that I had to try and join the Army."

"Well, thank you for that," came a less formal reply and tone. "Did you have anything in particular in mind that you wanted to do once you got into the Army? Or have you given that much thought up to this point?"

"I think I'd like to be a helicopter pilot... if that is possible."

"It is, but you have to pass some tests and a physical. Are you willing to do that?"

"Yes sir. Today... if it is possible."

"Where are you from, if I may ask? And does your family know you are here?"

"I'm from Fort Davis, Texas; and no Sir, they have no idea I'm here. It was my decision, and I wanted to come here as soon as I could."

"From Fort Davis?"

"No sir... from Alpine, Texas. I was attending Sul Ross State University up until yesterday. I rode the bus here yesterday and got in late last night."

"Well, then. If you've made up your mind about all this, we'll need to have you take a couple of pre-qualifying tests, answer some questions about your financial history, fill out some forms, and I'll do some quick background checks on you, and if you pass the tests and check out ok, then I'll have you go over to Fort Bliss, where they can give you the necessary preliminary physical and laboratory examinations. Once that is all done and you are found acceptable, then someone over there will swear you in. But you need to know that you're still a long way from starting actual pilot training for flying helicopters."

"How so?" E.B. interrupted.

"If you are qualified for entry, then you'll be assigned an Army installation where you will undergo the mandatory nine week Basic Combat Training course or BCT, as it is affectionately called. All new recruits are required to undergo this training, regardless of their eventual Military Occupational Specialty or MOS. This initial assignment for BCT will sometimes take up to 30 days, but in your case, seeing how you are hoping to have pilot training at Fort Rucker, they may reduce that waiting time. You'll need to leave me and the folks at Fort Bliss a reliable contact address and telephone number."

"I do need to tell you one thing," the once relieved but now increasingly anxious, new recruit stammered. "When I was in about the eleventh grade, I got arrested for taking building materials to build a club house for a group of my classmates. My dad let me go to jail to think about what I had done rather than post bail."

"Did you have any other problems like that afterwards?"

"No sir."

"Have you or did you take any illegal drugs?"

"No sir. Others did, but I didn't. But I did drink some beer when any of the other was going on."

"Well, then. I don't see too much to worry about. But I thank you for letting me know about that incident.

Most likely, it won't even show up on your county sheriff's rap sheet. But I need to check you out anyway.

"In the meantime, I'll have to sit over there," pointing to a small desk and armchair. "I will gather together the tests you are to take. There will be three distinct tests, which will probably take you all of two hours to complete. The first will be the Armed Forced Vocational Aptitude Battery or ASVAB, which contains six parts and these are to determine your enlistment eligibility and basic qualifications for particular military occupations. Of that test the last four sections make up the Armed Forces Qualification Test or AFQT. It, to me, is the real zinger of the bunch. It tests your arithmetic reasoning, mathematical knowledge, knowledge of words and paragraph comprehension. And the final test will be the Flight Aptitude Selection Test or FAST. You'll need to score 90 or higher on this to be eligible for pilot training."

Sitting down as directed, E.B.'s nervousness slowly increased. It didn't help that he had a poor night's sleep, but he was determined to follow through with this decision. He only hoped he would be qualified enough to be admitted into the Army. Taking a deep breath as the recruiter came over to the desk and laid out the tests, he stretched his arms, rolled his head and repositioned himself in the chair. He was about to begin one of the single most important tasks of his lifetime. Clearing his mind as much as possible, he began.

And as forewarned, it did take him all of two hours to complete the tests, which was about the same length of time it took the recruiter to make all the reference calls and background checks. They all gave E.B. glowing recommendations... remarkably. And most surprising of all, there was no indication on the police report of his ever being arrested or detained.

He was thrilled to learn that he scored a 93 on the AFQT, indicating that he was well above average in trainability. Likewise, he scored 92 on the FAST test, above the mandatory 90 level. It was clear he was an excellent candidate for volunteering to enter the Army.

"Ok." the sergeant finally looked up and addressed E.B. You did fine on your exams, and with everything I found out through my many telephone calls. Now it's time to take the next step."

"What's that?" E.B. asked somewhat concerned that it might involve another written test.

"I need to schedule you to go over to Fort Bliss, to their Military Entrance Processing Station or MEPS and take their physical and give them specimens for their laboratory tests. And if you pass all that, you will be sworn in today. How's that sound?"

"Great!" E.B. almost shouted. "I had no idea I could get all this done in one day."

"Well, we'll have to see if there is an opening before you get too excited. Do you want to get some coffee or have some breakfast while I get all this done. There's a coffee shop just down the street a ways. You may have passed it on the way here."

"Yes Sir, I remember passing it. When did you want me to return?"

"Give me an hour. Then if everything checks out, I'll arrange for transportation to Fort Bliss where they could swear you in today if everything checks out with your remaining tests and exams. You're just about three or four hours away from being a member of the United States Army."

The impact of hearing the sergeant say that stunned

E.B., but he managed to control his emotions enough to nod his head, turn and walk out of the office with a steady gait. And within thirty minutes the sergeant walked into the café, sat down beside E.B., nodded at the waitress that he would like to order something as well and told his newest recruit that the van would be there from the Army post in about 45 minutes.

Those next few hours at the MEPS, the ride back to Alpine on the bus and the shortened time frame of two weeks before he was to report to Fort Jackson in Columbia, South Carolina for his nine weeks of BCT became a blur. The time spent with Joan became steadily more precious, and it was clear to anyone who watched him carefully enough that his dance moves of yesteryear, essentially the jitterbug, were changing. It was like he was being caught up in a square dance hall. The multiple changes in his life mirrored the upcoming change of partners and dance moves associated with square dancing.

Even Joan noticed some changes occurring in that brief time. It was as if he were trying to protect her from what ordeals lay ahead for him, as well as prepare himself for the challenges that lay ahead. Whereas, he rarely drank much alcohol during the time they had been together, over the last week before he left for South Carolina on the bus, he began drinking more and more heavily. And with that he began to spend whatever money he had more freely. These, plus he seemed to become more aggressive with slights that may have happened by clerks, waitresses or friends. Likewise, his family noticed the same changes in his behavior. But it was easier for them to excuse it due to his recent enlistment.

To Joan it was puzzling, to say the least. But they agreed to work diligently on keeping in touch, trying to see each other whenever possible… such as her possibly coming to one of his graduation ceremonies and parades. And because his due date at Fort Jackson was September 31st, they anticipated that with his graduation from both the Warrant Officer Candidate School, followed by the extensive training leading to his becoming a Warrant Officer and getting his flight wings nine months later, she would plan on coming to Fort Rucker at the end of next June for his graduation.

That decided, they both felt more secure about the uncertain future that lay ahead for both of them. Joan was to finish her sophomore year at Sul Ross, while E.B. completed his flight training. She was then transferring to Texas A & M's Veterinarian Program for the next 3-4 years to study and prepare for becoming a large animal vet. And by the time she was done with that, they hoped to be able to marry and settle down somewhere, despite the likelihood for his overseas' deployments and her possible punishing job demands.

And by September 30th, the Columbia, South Carolina city bus dropped E.B. off at the embarkation point for all new Army recruits to be picked up by the Fort Jackson bus. His career was about to be launched. Surprisingly, Basic Training was not too physically taxing for him. There was a mental strain however. Growing up on a ranch, in the tiny town of Fort Davis, free from most of the quirks of having to interact with a bewildering cross-section of fellow Americans, even when a student at Sul Ross, he was unprepared for the conflicts and fights that arose daily in the barracks. But everyone in his training platoon soon learned that the lean and quiet Texan was no one to push too far. And soon he was recognized as a natural leader. But that was a role that E.B. did not seek nor embrace. He was by nature and circumstances a loner.

But a disturbing pattern began to emerge during the beginning of his new life far from home and Joan; he was beginning to take more risks. The opportunities to do so had not been as many or as exciting in his life previously. And it suited him to take them. It was something his cadre NCO's began to recognize as well. They weren't necessarily foolhardy risks, but they had the potential of being such. And as time passed, on a more subtle level, the risk-taking extended into beyond those initial weeks of Basic Training and later on during his initial pilot training, but risky behavior entered into his social interactions when he was not in uniform. He became more self-confident and what could only be described as flirtatious with both women in uniform and with the civilians he met on passes in the nearby communities. The worry that his superiors had was whether his risk taking was a kind of cover for deep-seated insecurities or whether it was the blossoming of someone who would have uncommon courage in stressful and hazardous situations. Only time would tell.

After the nine weeks of Basic Training and his stellar record achieved in all aspects of it, he was immediately transferred to Fort Rucker, Alabama to begin his six week warrant officer candidate school. Unlike pilots for fixed wing aircraft in the Air Force, Navy and Marine Corps, helicopter pilots for the Army can go from "High School to Flight School", provided they are willing and able to pilot helicopters with skill and courage. E.B. graduated at the top of his introductory warrant officer class.

He then began the actual training for becoming an Army Aviator. Initially, it involved intense classroom instruction prior to shifting to Fort Rucker's Warrior Hall, where the training switches to beginning to learn how to fly helicopters using a simulator. From there it was on to using the actual TH-67 training helicopter and finally making the last advance to becoming an expert pilot for one of four Army helicopters: those designed for reconnaissance, medical evacuations, transport or, the one E.B. gravitated to almost immediately upon seeing it on the tarmac, the one designed for attack... the AH-64 Apache. (see Appendix: **AH-64 Army Apache Helicopter**)

After long months of training and practice, it became clear to both E.B. and his superiors that he took to this aircraft like he was riding one of his newly broken horses on his family's Fort Davis ranch. Almost immediately, once he was allowed to solo in it, he left his instructors wide-eyed and open-mouthed as they watched him maneuver the aircraft. He was able to fly it backwards almost as fast as he could forward. He and the chopper were like a huge fish in or on top of the ocean... he could make it appear as if it were standing on its tail rotor and skim along the tops of imaginary waves like a porpoise. Or he could tip it on its nose and dive straight down like a falcon closing in on its prey. Soon it appeared as if the pilot and craft were in a kind of airborne ballet. His dance moves changed completely when he took control of it. It was a graceful and yet a potentially lethal thing to watch, because you knew that the firepower lurking within that machine could be so deadly against any foe. He became a unique example of someone who could dance both on the ground and in the air. And both would begin to define his character and course.

Despite E.B.'s graduation from pilot training and receiving his Army Aviator Badge in June of 2002, he still wasn't fully qualified for all phases of Apache chopper daylight and night combat support. To qualify for that he had to spend another three month period in maneuvers at Fort Irwin, California's National Training Center for desert combat and with the troops at Fort Polk, Louisiana for Joint National Training.. Afterwards, he would be fully qualified to be stationed either in Iraq or Afghanistan.

But these were concerns for the future. What concerned him most, despite the various semi-serious dalliances he had over the last ten months with brief passes into the communities around Fort Rucker and some weekends in Panama City, Florida and Mobile, Alabama, each within a 100 to 125 mile radius of his duty station, was seeing Joan again. For someone nineteen, going on twenty, he tried to excuse himself with drifting a bit when it came to meeting young women his age. And yet he wondered if Joan was having the same temptations. She was, after all, a strikingly beautiful and intelligent individual. Leaving aside his periodic doubts about himself and her, he was extremely excited about seeing her. His sister Nin was going to try to make it for his graduation ceremony, but neither of his parents could make it. His father was too tied up with ranch chores and his mother had just had major surgery for correction of a faulty heart valve. Happily, Joan was arriving two days before the graduation and staying a week.

It was a time of great joy for all three. Nin only stayed two days, but reconnecting with her brother was a delight for him and for Joan. And because E.B. was given ten days leave before starting his last phase of training, he and Joan went to New Orleans for a week.

At the end of that time he had to give her the news that his company commander had given him just before he left for leave. And that was that once he completed his last three months of training, he would be assigned to the 1st Air Cavalry Division stationed at Fort Hood, Texas and from there would certainly be shipped to somewhere in the Middle East for a twelve month deployment.

And as promised, his stay at Fort Hood was brief because on March 2, 2003, he and others in his combat aviation brigade, known officially as the "Air Cavalry Brigade", were issued orders to depart immediately to Kuwait, and from there they would be assigned Apache helicopters to coordinate with the ground and armored troops sweeping into Iraq and on into Baghdad.

His was the first of 17,000 soldiers of the 1st Cavalry Division to be shipped over. The entire division was deployed in January, 2004 to the Baghdad region, essentially to replace the 1st Armored Division. And while his Division was deployed again in November, 2006 to December, 2007 and in January, 2009 to January 2010, his group of aviators was sent again in 2005 for another year. In other words, he had two years of overseas combat duty involving battles in Baghdad, Fallujah, Al Kut, Karbala and Balad before his full Division had returned for their second tour. And while in those areas, it was not uncommon for him to witness the mammoth sand storms that swept across Iraq's landscape. They were called "haboob's". (see Appendix: **Haboob**). They were one of the very few natural phenomena or sights he saw in those stressful years that impressed him. Beyond them, there was just the blur of war.

And then after this second year's deployment, he got orders to report to Fort Bliss to join up with the 1st Armored Division which was being transferred there in its entirety from its home base in Germany. He was to be assigned to the "Iron Eagle" Aviation Brigade, with its headquarters at Fort Bliss' Biggs Army Airfield. No reassignment could have made him happier. At last he and Joan could begin to make definite plans for their future together.

She had just completed her Veterinary Medicine Program and had passed her Texas State Board of Veterinary Medicine examination and was then fully qualified to practice large animal veterinary medicine about the same time E.B. flew into Fort Bliss. Not having taken any short leaves mid-deployment, he was now entitled to thirty days off, which he intended to fully use for their marriage in Houston and for their honeymoon. After their honeymoon, they would establish their home residence in Alpine, where Joan was joining an existing practice. From there E.B. would commute on a weekly basis back and forth to Fort Bliss for the next year... or at least until his next inevitable return to either Iraq or Afghanistan.

It was clear to Joan that E.B. had changed from all his exposure to combat, even if it was at an accelerated speed and zooming over the battle in a dizzying display of aerial acrobatics. He well deserved his rank of Chief Warrant Officer Three (CW3), and everyone, except her, now called him "Chief". He was becoming a legend in the theater and at home throughout all the Services. He would go into a raging battle, twisting, darting, barrel-rolling, fairly dancing in mid-air, often saving the ground troops below from additional casualties. His dance steps now were a combination of his youthful jitterbug combined with a full-blown break dance routine, with its stunning spinning, flipping over and backwards gyrations. He was a master of the skies; even jet fighter pilots marveled at how he maneuvered his Apache craft at such low altitudes. It defied all the laws of physics.

But, more ominously to Joan, all this exposure to danger and a world of constant threat and death had transformed him, albeit she hoped for only a temporary period. Granted, he was now an uncommonly courageous soldier, one who seemed to hold death in contempt by his bold actions, and he had a uniform overflowing with medals of valor, easily displaying to any passersby that he had been duly honored for living through fierce struggles. But underlying all this color and the well-deserved recognition was an undercurrent of anger. And it above all was the one thing that she needed to get exposed: why was her sweet, sophomore college student of 2001 now verging on becoming lost within almost bubbling rage? She would not allow it to happen. She vowed she would reverse the emotional toll that a terribly expensive and puzzling war in a region beset by countless millennia of constant war and a total lack of self-control or self-government was causing to permanently alter and embitter her husband. It might take time and much love, but she knew him well enough to know even this most lethal of wounds could be healed.

Possibly some of his anger was the result of disappointment, but she seriously doubted that, given that he had enlisted voluntarily and flying was the other love of his life... besides her. And she did not sense he had any resentment toward the military itself; nor of the personnel he served with; nor more personally with her or their getting married. It seemed to bubble forth more when he was in a civilian setting, when he was stationed back in the States. It seemed related to the changes he was becoming more and more aware of in the culture around him. And it seemed to be a kind of protective response, something related to the unspoken and mysterious realm of the informal brotherhood of his fellow men. And the more she thought about it, she realized this resentment was most likely unrelated to his successes and achievements, but more because of the lack of them for his civilian male counterparts. He was becoming the victim of a cultural backlash, one rooted in a fundamentally reactionary rant heard in closeted conversations nationwide; it concerned what some claim was the feminization of America and the apparent downsizing and marginalizing of so many men in the country. She was sure he was suffering from a kind of culture shock.

Sensing that this was at the heart of much of his mood changes, at least more so than any battlefield fatigue or a well deserved traumatic stress disorder, she felt being sheltered in a home of love and kindness would eventually begin to expose the unnecessary, cultural baggage that he was carrying. He was too good a man to let some manhood-cult obsession overwhelm him. And with those thoughts behind her, she eagerly embraced the Chief; and they began their life together at last. Even E.B., for all he had seen and done over these last five years knew something so grand and wondrous had entered his life: a loving and precious woman. His square dance days were over. She was to be his sole partner to the end.

And fortunately for him, even though he did have another two tours back to the Middle East... both of them returns to Iraq... the fighting there had markedly decreased with each tour. In those next five years, ending in 2011, when the drawdown of American troops in Iraq was completed, a grim total of over 4,500 American troops were killed and over 32,000 were seriously wounded with the additional loss of 75 helicopters, 36 of which were lost to enemy fire. Changed forever, as he left Iraq after that last tour, he knew his days of skillful and lethal dancing were over. He had somehow survived.

Finally, come April, 2011, he was given an assignment that would not entail the annual deployments back into Theater. He was promoted to being a brigade supervisor of an Army helicopter unit at Ramstein Air Base in Germany. Joan and their son, Eliot, were to relocate with him as well. She was to take an extended sabbatical leave from her practice in Alpine, and when this tour of duty was over, E.B. had mentioned that he might like to return to his family's ranch and see if he could make it prosper again. As it turned out, none of his sisters were interested in staying on there permanently. For Joan, his decision was a clear signal that the healing process was underway.

THE ASSEMBLING

THIRTEEN: AL HABOOB

The introductory meeting with the masked-covered individuals, who Inti knew only as al Haboob, was held late one afternoon on a typical, mixed rain and snow showers Saturday in early January, 2012. He had been asked by someone that same day after the first morning prayers to be at a particular payphone down the street from where he lived at exactly 10:30 a.m., and wait there for a call. Further, he was to wear a full-length overcoat and carry an umbrella, which seemed natural to Inti, given the foul weather they were having. And he was to follow the instructions given him as to the exact times and places that were provided. No deviation could be allowed. From this point on he must act and behave like his every move could be monitored or that he was being followed. The success or failure of his mission depended entirely upon his stealth and composure at all times.

Because the telephone was on the Blvd. St. Michel, and it was constantly being used by pedestrians and passersby, there was nothing in particular out of the order for Inti to happen to be walking by just as it rang once.

Glancing around nonchalantly to make sure he didn't appear to be noticed picking up the phone just as it rang, he picked it up and said, "Yes?"

The voice on the other end replied, "Someone has just slipped instructions into your overcoat pocket while you were distracted answering this call. Follow them... starting right now!", and then the call was disconnected.

Looking down at his overcoat, on the side that he had been holding the telephone receiver, there was now a piece of paper sticking out of the pocket. Not wanting to appear too obvious, he nonchalantly strolled over to a vacant storefront doorway and pretended to fumble inside his coat for something. Eventually, he reached into the pocket with the message in it. On it was written:

"Step forward onto the curb in front of you and hail a taxi. Give the driver the instructions to take you to Bibliotheque nationale de France's main entrance, which is located on 11 Quai Francois Mauriac. Once you arrive there, enter the building and go immediately through it to the north exit and walk across that street and wait to catch the #24 bus. Have the driver drop you off at the Nogent-sur-Marne intersection at Bois de Vincennes. Exit the bus there and walk into the garden's Avenue de Nogent street entrance. About 100 meters inside the gate and on the left hand side of that street will be a collection of park benches. Behind them is a small grove of trees. Secured to one of those trees is a bicycle. In this note you will find a key to the lock. Under the seat is a small plastic bag with an address written on a small piece of paper. Memorize the address, but then you must swallow the paper. NO ONE IS TO SEE THAT ADDRESS!! NO ONE!!! Then ride the bike to Avenue de Fortenay, onto Ave. du President Roosevelt, then on to Rue Maurice Couderchet and finally onto Rue Mot. Find the large green apartment complex across the street from Ecole Maternelle Mot. Go to Apt. 237 and knock two times… wait… then knock five times more. Now… you are to swallow this message as well. Go! We will be waiting for you."

By the time he reached the designated address, cold and wet, it was 1:15 p.m. Pausing at the door to apartment 237, he tried to recall the sequence of knocks he was supposed to use. Eventually, he thought he recalled the exact number and knocked as described.

Within only a few seconds afterwards, the heavy wooden door, which looked like it had been painted over countless times, opened and there before him in the crack of the doorway was an individual with a face-covering balaclava, with only the eyes and mouth showing.

"Enter! Quickly now." came the voice heavily accented French with what seemed to Inti to be possibly some Arabic or more likely some Farsi accent. "Please, if you will, take a seat at the far end of the table," the raspy male voice added as the door was closed as soon as he entered the darkened room.

The only light was from a small table lamp, placed in the middle of a six-to-seven foot long table. There appeared to be no other furnishings in the room aside from that table and the six chairs, four of which were presently occupied with more masked-face individuals.

Once Inti had removed his soaked overcoat and shook it to remove the remnants of some powdery snow that had just started to fall prior to his turning his bicycle onto Rue Mot, he sat in the arm chair that had been indicated he use. While he was doing so, the figure who met him at the door was seating himself at the other end of the table. The stage was now set for unquestionably the gravest and most significant conversation that was to occur in the history of humanity. It and what followed in the months to come were to alter entirely the course of history... like none others. And it began with an uncommon formality and reserve, both of which when Inti looked back on the occasion, he was puzzled at the grace and politeness that can proceed such a massive, incomparable event.

"We will not be introducing ourselves to you out of concern for your own safety and ours. But we will provide you the evidence you need to have that we are who we say we are, and to assure you that those of us gathered here will be your stalwart companions and security detail throughout what you are about to undertake. One or more of the five of us will ALWAYS be providing security for you at any one time from this day forward. And each of us will also serve as the necessary workers you will need to complete your upcoming mission.

"However, from this moment on, no one is ever to know of our existence or what we discuss now or ever with you. Do you understand that?"

Still breathless from his long bicycle ride and then climbing the stairs to this apartment, Inti could only nod his head and whisper, "Yes I do. I understand. But what is it that you have in mind for me to do? I have no idea what all this is about."

"Good," came the reply from the same speaker at the other end of the table. "That ignorance is exactly what there has to be for ANYONE outside this room. And now I will tell you why and what we are going to do... you and the five of us."

And with the discussion that followed, ninety-nine percent of it being dominated by the five masked individuals in the room, one of whom had a feminine voice, Inti became woven into a plot of staggering proportions. And midway through the presentation, he realized that he had no choice other than to agree to join them. No one could hear what they were telling him and expect to live, if he or she decided to abandon them or this mission.

Over time, he began to speak more, mainly inquiring about procedural matters, timelines and logistical operations. And to his amazement, there did not appear to be any flaws in what they had conceived, other than the bold assumption that he could somehow manage to participate in the design and manufacture of what they envision he could.

But like the scientist that he was, he immediately began the process of analyzing the practicality or feasibility of each aspect of their plan. Finally, after a long pause of absolute quiet while he scratched some numbers and drew some diagrams on a notepad that they had previously placed in front of him, he looked up and stared purposefully at each individual and said, "I do believe it can be done. I will be honored to join your band of warriors."

And then the five masked individual rose, signaling to him that he should do the same, and together they all recited: "to victory, to a more perfect world and to paradise. May God protect and guide us, as his instrument of peace through conquest, we the members of al Haboob."

There were hugs and the shaking of hands all around the table after that and then an agreement for all of them to meet together at their next staging area: Qum, Iran, two months from that day. And thereafter each individual in the room left at a different time, to avoid looking like they somehow knew one another. And before each left the room, they removed their head coverings, but it was as they faced the door, so Inti never saw their faces. He was the next to the last to leave, with the individual who met him at the door initially the last one to exit. And when he got to the street there was no sign of any of the others. They simply disappeared in the rain and snowy dusk of a wintry Paris.

And for Inti, the initial strains of a new dance, of Dance Macabre, could now be heard faintly echoing around him… if he or anyone else would take the time and effort to listen. It's usually not heard, at least at first, by the individual who is at its source; that's because anyone associated with its beginning also has developed a tone deafness to anything but the chorus of chants that sing his praises. That and it isn't a musical melody that appeals to them as much as it is the movement … the rhythm. And this dance had a drum beat that was hypnotizing to Inti. It lured him out into the darkening evening enveloped in a spell of self-satisfaction and with a gloating assurance of the justified revenge to come.

And this dance does happen. And sadly, it happens all too often when the dance steps that men choose are those that appear to elevate their sense of absolute manhood above and beyond whatever dances others around them are struggling to master. The dance steps for a good and decent life are not simple nor are they particularly fashionable or attention- getting. They're not automatically learned just through the ongoing, inevitable aging process. And they are certainly not attained through the myriad manhood rituals that have become mandatory for youth, seeking to enter the adult world.

And most certainly any musical accompaniment to this particular dance that Inti was about to initiate should have been a warning to others, and if it was not heeded, it would soon become a dirge.

FOURTEEN: THE PLAN UNFOLDS

Inti didn't arrive back at his home until about two hours later. He essentially backtracked the same way he came to this all-important meeting. And when he walked in, Froncett was visibly upset, because she had no idea where he'd been nor when he would return. It was not like him to be so thoughtless, and then his reaction to her beginning to chide him confused her further. He almost immediately became enraged at her questioning him as to his whereabouts and the hour of his return. But even more curious to her was when their children entered the living room, his mood changed completely to one of a doting father. And yet prior to this confrontation, Froncett had seen a few other puzzling reactions and changes in him that were to only become magnified over the next eleven months.

The next surprise was when he announced mid-week that he had been notified that he could take his six month sabbatical earlier than she and he had discussed. It was always their plan to spend some time in the Rhone River Valley of Switzerland, while he commuted back and forth to the Large Hadrom Collider near Geneva. However, that too was changed. Next, he told her that before beginning that phase of his sabbatical, he first wanted to travel alone to Pakistan and study the evolution of their nuclear energy and nuclear weapons programs. He hoped what he learned there could be adapted to other developing countries, especially as everyone needed a cheaper energy source and more of it. He added that he hoped to then travel more extensively throughout the underdeveloped world helping to set up these programs.

When Froncett asked when he planned on leaving, again to her surprise he told her in about two weeks, that the French Atomic Energy Commission was granting this absence, as long as he came back for a few weeks thereafter to finish whatever he was currently investigating. Then he and the family would head to Switzerland for the last four months of his sabbatical.

Following this surprising announcement, he added an equally puzzling request of her. He suggested that she might get a little friendlier with the various national government ministers and their families when they are admitted to her hospital for care. He said it would be nice to extend their circle of friends and begin socializing more. He'd never showed much interest in her work before or in her associates or patients. But after some thought, she decided that maybe he was hoping to branch out once his sabbatical was completed and try to go into business for himself. He was simply trying to establish a business network. And when she suggested this was his reason, he readily agreed and thanked her for her insight and willingness to help with this request.

The two weeks went by so fast that Froncett was uncommonly stunned when Inti announced that he would be departing the next day at 7 a.m. for Karachi, Pakistan. Further, it shocked her to see how little he was packing for him to be gone for the next two months. Everything he packed easily fit into a small carry-on bag. It appeared to her that he was packing for just a weekend trip. But Inti reassured her that he didn't really have the clothes to wear in the climate he would be studying and working in. Whatever he needed, he would get over there. It all seemed far too practical of him for her to believe entirely everything he said. She basically had to purchase everything he presently owned, and she had to police everything he put on for any occasion. Without question, she knew he had the worst taste in clothing than anyone on the planet.

But come 4:30 a.m. the next day, he was dressed and packed and insisted that she not accompany him to the airport. It was too dark and dreary. He'd just catch a taxi. Passing through the various security checkpoints was no problem for him. He was previously instructed at the al Haboob meeting two weeks earlier not to pack much. Whatever he needed would be provided him, once he landed in Karachi.

The flight itself took over nineteen hours, with one stopover in Cairo, Egypt. It was only the second time in his life that he had flown anywhere, and given the circumstances of his taking the trip and his novice status as a traveler, he was becoming uncharacteristically unnerved. And as much as his faith forbade him from drinking any alcohol, he was becoming overpowered with the temptation. Fortunately for him, the flight ended with him sleeping the last five hours before landing.

Once he cleared customs, there was someone waiting for him who was holding up a sign. It simply had "Inti" printed on it in big letters. Without a word from his escort, he was motioned to follow him to a waiting car, which was jammed in amongst a surging mass of other vehicles of all sizes, shapes and colors, traveling at speeds that defied any logical person's concept of safety and courtesy. And after a thirty minute drive, he was driven up to a modest building in the far west side of the city. There was still no conversation with the driver. He simply got out and opened the back car door to let Inti out and then motioned for him to go up the steps to the building's front door.

It was an overly crowded neighborhood, much like the ones he used to pass in La Paz coming and going to the Mosque from the University. A dusty pall hung over the city and area, with the streets littered with the telltale signs of an impoverished and overcrowded urban landscape, one that exists in two-thirds of the world. Inti shook his head as he knocked on the heavy metal, security door; thinking as he did 'maybe… just maybe… what we are planning will change the way so much of our world lives, believes and thinks. A wake-up call is coming'. And then the door opened just slightly and someone inside asked.

"Your name, please sir?" in a voice that seemed somewhat familiar.

"My name is Inti Menani, and what may I ask is yours?"

Opening the door wide enough to allow Inti to enter, the cautious inquirer replied, "At this moment it is unimportant, and neither is your old name, which from this moment whenever you are fully involved in the sacred mission that you now are on; it is to be Philip D'Mone. You are never to use your another name at any time you are out of France or whenever you are doing vital business involving the mission. Do you understand, Monsieur D'Mone?"

Baffled, but beginning to realize by his decision to go along with the members of the al Haboob that he was entering a secret world exhaustively preparing for an extremely lethal mission. In response, he nodded his head and simply replied, "Oui, monsieur."

"Très bien...entrer, si vous plaît," came the crisp acknowledgement that Inti understood immediately as to the need for strict adherence to his new identity.

Once inside the dingy apartment, the individual at the door motioned Inti to sit down at a small table by the front window. As he was doing so, the curiously familiar figure spoke with the same Middle Eastern French accent, which Inti recognized immediately from that day two weeks ago, "We met in the room on Rue Mot. I was sitting directly in front of you."

"I thought so," Inti replied, contrasting the speaker's speech with his own nearly perfect French, long tested and polished since his Freshman Year at La Paz University. "I recognized your voice right away at the front door."

"For the purpose of our trip and for the remainder of these next eleven months together off and on, you may call me 'Jon'," the tall, muscular fellow advised.

He had a noticeably lighter complexion than was usual for someone from North Africa or the western portion of the Middle East. Inti was puzzled as to where he actually was from, so he asked, "Are you originally from this area?"

"No," Jon answered. "I was born in Iran, and I spent the first twenty-two years there. After that, I transferred to the University of Paris branch in Nice to study mechanical engineering. My specialty is metallurgy. But on the journey we are about to start in approximately thirty minutes, you and I are both exploratory geologists. We have been invited by the Government of Afghanistan to survey their western region for the presence of minerals that can be refined into precious metals."

"But I know absolutely nothing about that subject," Inti protested.

"Never mind that. Neither do I... for the most part," Jon answered. "But whatever we do know far exceeds what any border guard or military personnel at a random roadblock might know."

"But what about credentials? Visas? Identification?" Inti interrupted.

"I have all that right here on the table," Jon replied, as the soon-to-be-the-expedition-driver sat down across from him. "And now I will explain what is ahead for us in the two week timeline we have to reach the Iranian border, where we will then be met by officials of their government who will escort us to Fordo, twenty miles north of Qum. And for now that's really about all you need to know."

What followed was a series of instructions and various contingency plans for the trip ahead. And within the period of time Jon had specified earlier, he was finished talking and requested Inti now rise and exit through the back door of the apartment. Once outside, he led him to a seemingly new four-wheel drive, all-terrain Range Rover SUV. The back seat and luggage area were packed full with boxes and various scientific instruments. It was clear to Inti that this undertaking had the most thorough planning and vetting. These were no amateurs that he was going to be working with. Many months or, more likely... years ...had gone into organizing and planning this mission.

And just before Jon started the vehicle, as they both fastened their seat belts, he handed Inti his new passport.

"Please give me your other passport. I'll return it to you prior to your flight back to Paris. This new one is the one you will use until then. Please practice saying your new name and don't EVER forget it whenever you are with me or any of the others in our cadre."

Inti only nodded as he took it from him. The realization of what he was embarking on now hit him full force. Even if he wanted to, which he didn't, there was no turning back from this well-coordinated plan. And with the formalities aside, Jon started the vehicle, and they drove out of Karachi on National Highway 25 or N-25, as the locals call it, through Quetta, heading toward Chamman on the Pakistan-Afgan border. From there, they drove on to Kandahar, a total of 903 kilometers or about 560 miles from Karachi. If all went well, it would only take them about two to three days to make that leg of the trip, but Jon had allowed them one week, given the terrain and the customary stoppages and unexpected events that occur in this part of the world.

Crossing into Afghanistan at Spin Boldak wasn't nearly the tense experience that Inti imagined it might be. Their passports and all the scientific gear that they were carrying, along with a forged document from the Afgan Interior Ministry, paved the way for them to pass almost unheeded through customs. From there, the trip was to take them through Herat and due west to the Iranian border, a distance of about 780 kilometers or 500 miles. It was through some of the most heavily infested area of Talaban insurgents. And certainly roadside bombs and mines could be an every-present hazard. But from what Jon told him, their passage through this area was guaranteed, given the importance of their mission. Their vehicle had been well described to all who might otherwise wish them harm. And two days before their two week deadline, they arrived at the Iranian border crossing.

It had been a long and often uncomfortably cold trip. Inti was not conditioned for this kind of activity. His life since his University days had been cushioned and secluded. Hardship and discomfort were alien to him since his childhood and adolescent years. But he tried not to complain. Jon was attentive and tried to ease his discomfort as much as possible. Their long road journey was only days from completion, and he had been told that he would be flown out of Tehran back to Karachi once they were finished with their mission in Qum. However, there had not been much detail provided as to exactly why they were coming all this way to Iran. He sensed in the broadest terms possibly why, as it was outlined in his meeting with the other four members of the team in Paris four weeks earlier. But who they would meet and why specifically they were coming into Iran was still a mystery, even up to the time they easily crossed the border.

It was as if the border guards had been forewarned that they would be coming. And in fact, Inti had seen Jon remove something resembling a cell phone when they had their last stop in Afghanistan, but it was by mutual understanding that neither of them would bother the other when they stopped to rest and eat. They spent enough time with each other as it was. Most often Inti would eat by himself, being completely unfamiliar with the people of either country they were traveling through. On the other hand, his companion often ate with other people. He was gregarious and apparently spoke several languages. At the end of each of these stops he told Inti that he did this socializing on purpose. It was a way to spread the word that they were exploratory geologists. It was a way he sought to maintain their cover and not arouse suspicion.

Crossing the Iranian border was anticlimactic, given the remarkable terrain they went through to cross from Pakistan into Afghanistan. Neither of them were searched or asked any questions. The border guards did ask to see their passports, but that was the end of the inspection. There then followed a three hour wait just on the inside of the border crossing, but out of sight of any Afghani soldiers or policemen. In fact, when the black limousine pulled up to escort them into the country, they were told to leave their vehicle behind. It was no longer needed. And apparently Iranian authorities did arrive some time later to drive it away to an undisclosed location.

The trip through Khohasan and Semnan Provinces was unnervingly dull and long. They passed through the towns of Täybad, Torbat-e, Mashad, Sabsevär and Shahrüd into Tehran. From there they had to drive south to Qum. They only stopped for fuel and food, but only when it was absolutely necessary. And no one spoke... not one word the entire trip. As he was to learn later, their escort was circumventing Dasht-e Lut, a massive desert region of over 360,000 square miles. This last road trip for Inti was to be 800 miles. And the only verbal exchange was at the Tehran city limits where their passports were checked again. Then silence ensued until they reached Qum. It was one of the worst experiences of Inti's life. The boredom was almost unbearable. He had no books to read, no paper to write on. He just sat and looked out the window at countryside devoid of any interesting or pleasant scenery.

Arrival in Qum was highlighted by their being dropped off at a comfortable hotel and told to take the rest of the day and night off, that the next day would bring an entourage of military and government officials to meet with them. Inti assumed the latter group would be primarily religious clerics or their representatives.

What followed next was a week of intense meetings, traveling back and forth to Fordo, where Natanz, was the site for ongoing, highly secret scientific activity. About two days into that week, Inti was surprised to see the four remaining members of al Haboob join the group of scientists and engineers. And, upon his finally getting to see each of their faces, he was able to learn of their particular training and skills. The remaining four individuals were respectively a chemical engineer, a structural engineer and a mechanical engineer, with the one woman on the team being a logistics specialist. And all of them had extensive military training, as he was eventually to learn. Each, as it turned out, was from a different country, all of which bordered the Mediterranean Sea. One was an Egyptian, one a Palestinian, another a Moroccan, and the woman was from Algeria, just as Froncett had been. They were each highly qualified in their respective fields, and there was no question in Inti's mind that this group had the highest clearance for what they were about to see hidden in a top secret vault deep within a nearby mountain range. It had to be held in strictest secrecy. The preplanning for this project had undoubtedly taken years. He was sure of that now, seeing what was unfolding around him. It made him proud to be included. Any reservations he had about what was being planned and developed were disappearing with each passing day. His faith and beliefs were firm and his resolve became unshakable.

It's only by the most unlikely of chances that you, the reader, are now privy to this entire story. Without the series of leaks, confessions, interrogations and the resulting interventions and invasions, this material would never have reached the public. Even now as it is being digested and exposed, there are gaps in the information and which individuals were involved. Only time and more diligence will reveal the full story of the characters immediately and peripherally involved, such as Colin, E.B. and their families.

And once the overall review, final plan and methodology were agreed upon, Inti and his group split off and began the process of what was needed to assemble something an unknown host of groups and possibly nations had conceived. At last it was time to begin fabrication. It took over a month of their working around the clock to preassemble the project to enough that Inti could leave and return to Paris. In all likelihood, his expertise was no longer needed beyond that point. The next phase of his involvement would not be necessary until some months later. And besides, he had to be back by the end of the agreed upon, two month period or suspicions would certainly be aroused. All but one of his five associates was to stay behind, and then one by one the remainder would eventually to catch up with him as the deadline approached.

His solo flight in a government transport plane from Tehran to Karachi was uneventful. It landed at a military airfield and was essentially an unrecorded flight and delivery. There was no record of it having ever occurred. It was necessary for him to return to Karachi at the point of departure for Paris. His passport had to show he had entered and exited this port of entry to verify his previously agreed upon two month sabbatical period there.

When he finally arrived back home in Paris, he was greeted by a hostile Froncett. Not once had he communicated with her or his family over the entire two month period. And there had been some discussion prior to his leaving Iran within the al Haboob team about what her reaction would most likely be due to this long-term silence. None of the other five members were married, and they were each concerned that although it was necessary for his long-term cover to be non-communicative during his time away, they also knew he was likely to have a major issue arise from this time away. And likewise they were concerned he would have the same issue to face given the other operational demands which would be necessary prior to the time everything could be concluded. That initial confrontation had arrived.

"I do apologize so sincerely," Inti began. Now it was time for him to begin dancing neither without any musical accompaniment nor with any particular dance rhythm or style. Such a dance is the one invariable dictated by the manhood ritual when deceit, lying and betrayal are necessary for self-preservation, and when the false front of unfaithfulness is at hand. And this, too, is another aspect of the impregnator's persona. In order to fulfill the demands of this particular ritual and to gain full membership, there has to be unfaithfulness and cheating. It is part of the thrill of the hunt: developing the overconfidence associated with achieving machismo. In short, acquiring this sense of accomplishment at taking these kinds of risks means any dancing possible now is all in your head. You have excluded all sense of loyalty, faithfulness and the need to be trusted. Your manhood ritual has placed you on a self-styled pedestal. But Inti knew he now had to fabricate amends. He needed Froncett and the family to complete this mission.

"I have been thoughtless and I know I have appeared unloving, but you must know that I treasure you above all else in my life," he continued. "Scientists are notorious for immersing themselves in their work and leaving all around them to guess what they are thinking and doing."

"But why me? Why have you been so presumptuous with me? We have always prided ourselves on being a team, united in our efforts to have a family and create a life for them and for ourselves. Is there someone else in your life? Do you have a mistress?"

"On everything that is holy, I can swear there is no one else but you," he affirmed, thinking at the same time that he was relieved she hadn't said 'something'. I have just gotten so involved in the science of what I am doing, I've become distracted and aloof. Please, please forgive me. The most taxing part of this new discovery of mine and of its implementation is now past, so we can now begin to really enjoy our lives together. I am done with this need for separation and the demand for total concentration."

"Are you sure? You'd better be. I cannot work and raise three children on my own, and it's certainly not what we agreed would happen when we became engaged."

"THREE! What do you mean 'three'? He gasped.

"I was going to surprise you with the news," she replied.

"What news?"

"I am pregnant with our third child."

He had to gather himself, because this was not what he had expected… far from it. This news caused him to have some instant hesitation. His zeal and commitment to the upcoming surprise he and the members of the al Haboob were planning became less urgent and almost problematic.

"When is our baby due?" he tried to ask with at least a modest amount of eagerness and delight.

"I found out three days ago, when I went to our family physician. I'm a little over two months pregnant. She tells me our baby is due around the middle of September.

"That's such wonderful news," he continued to emote, trying desperately not to show his shock and confusion. Adding to this sudden surprise of Froncett's was that he and his cohorts had scheduled their package to be delivered in December sometime; depending on how successful the remaining stages of the plan proceeded, according to the schedule outline he and his team had developed. But attempting to thrust all these mixed emotions aside, he came forward and kissed her gently, and they hugged. His first step in creating an atmosphere of fidelity and trust had begun. And it was with some relief that he let out a deep sigh at her unreserved response to his apparent contrition and pleasure at her news. She in turn hugged him back and felt somewhat chided at being so judgmental.

As he had promised his supervisors at the facility in Valduc, he returned the next Monday and gave them a brief fabrication of his findings and work in Pakistan. He then asked if he could proceed within the next week to moving his family and himself to Geneva and finish the remainder of his four month sabbatical. And during this time he would begin to groom Froncett into wanting to meet socially with the Government Ministers that she had as patients. These contacts were central to the success of his mission. And if possible, the social interactions must begin even while they are on the remainder of his sabbatical.

And thus began the second act in Inti's faux dance routine: that pretending tenderness, loving affection and deep concern for his family, all the while harboring a deceit of unimaginable consequences. His recurrent apologies and proclamations of earnest love seemed to win over Froncett's skepticism about his motives and intentions towards her and their children. His pretense was convincing, and she readily joined unknowingly into the midst of this second dance... even though she was not actually his partner. Deceit was. She was simply a pawn.

In that vein, the back and forth communication that Froncett had with the wives of three of the Cabinet Ministers began to bear fruit. She and Inti were invited to four formal events and then to two very informal ones involving dinner and drinks that lasted far into the night. Two of the black tie events occurred while they were still staying in Geneva. They had to leave their children with their nanny who was a full time resident and had been since they had their first child. With both their salaries, it had not been a problem to hire and keep one. And having her immediately available at all times allowed them mobility to attend conferences and parties at will.

But come the middle of June, it was time for Inti and his family to return to Paris from Geneva. His sabbatical was over. And now they had to face what every Parisian abhors... a summer in Paris with the flood of all the tourists and the stifling heat. And during the summer months, it is commonplace for the government officials to head south to the French Riviera, but not the Minister of Interior and the Lord Mayor of Paris and their families... at least not this summer. And Inti and Froncett were becoming regular guests in their home or at designated times in various restaurants along the Avenue des Champs-Elysées. The entire Grand Plan of Inti's and the al Haboob was working better than anyone had hoped or expected. The special request he needed to make for access was not over a couple of months away now. And then Inti would be entering his third and final dance phase.

And while he was taking care of the necessary business in Paris, the four remaining associates were toiling frantically to follow his book-length instructions that he left them after their clandestine, month-long time together. The fifth member of al Haboob always remained in the shadows, watching and guarding Inti's every move. Getting the necessary supplies often took longer than the various Iranian authorities promised they would. And some items had to be purchased on the black market far beyond Iranian borders. It was an undertaking involving many hundreds of unaware individuals or companies across the globe. But the focal point of it all still lay in the recesses of a sealed laboratory in Fordo, Iran, 20 miles north of Qum. Eventually, however, by the end of October, the product was completed and ready for delivery. And it was at this point that the other four members of al Haboob began to separate, only to reassemble again in Paris in December. It was Jon who was selected to go first and make contact with Inti. The clock was now set and had begun ticking… it was December 11th, when he flew out of Tehran.

FIFTEEN: ONWARD TO PARIS

Colin made reservations to stay in one of the more traditional hotels along the Avenue des Champ-Elysées. It would provide a great staging area for wherever the family wanted to go for the week they were there. And they would drive over from Kew, using the Chunnel. It would add to the adventure of the trip. He was sure it would be a great adventure for Zackary as well. And happily, the indiscretions of two years ago were not discussed and fumed over as often now, and there was a certain degree of trust returning to his and Jill's marriage. She had even begun expressing eager anticipation of their trip. They were to leave Kew at 7:30 a.m. on December 18th and planned on registering at the hotel by 5 p.m.

Besides their making the mandatory tour of the various museums and the Eiffel Tower, Jill wanted to take a cruise up the Seine. She felt it would be so romantic, and Colin wholeheartedly agreed. To do so, he arranged to have them have a late lunch cruise on what turned out to be a rather large private yacht. It would depart from its mooring on the south side of the river about a mile west of the Eiffel Tower. Its outlined route was to sail up river well past the Isle de la Cite, and the return back past their embarkation point for another three to five miles. It would take all of four hours due to pauses for the passengers to take photographs, boarding tourists at other wharfs and the yacht simply sailing slowly to allow the visitors to gaze at the beauty around them.

The vessel's name was Le Lointain Horizon, The Distant Horizon, and the pictures of her in the brochure they sent Jill were stunning. It had a very large open deck both for and aft, with almost floor to ceiling windows in the dining room, which was situated on the main deck in-between the two open deck areas. Undoubtedly, reclining chairs were placed on the deck in the Spring and Summer; but for it being mid-winter, there were only a couple of them on the aft deck. And below this main deck there was a small stage and dance area. It looked like the perfect vessel for them to take a tour on, and it would certainly be the highlight of their vacation. And of course, Zackary would be with them, as well, during this sight-seeing excursion.

When the day came to start their vacation, Colin had been so excited that he had their car packed two days in advance. Nothing could stop them from going, and come the morning of December 18th, they entered the traffic flow into the Chunnel and soon were in France. The week was like the honeymoon that they never had, given their having to continue with their studies in Brisbane and work at that time.

Their vacation pace was relaxed, and there was even snow their third day in Paris. The next day it was colder, as is always the case once a winter storm front passes through. But by Christmas Eve day, the weather had moderated enough that taking the boat ride on the Seine, even in the late afternoon, was almost perfect. The snow still outlined the roofs of the city. Everywhere you looked it was another postcard picture in the making. Paris was resplendent for one of the most holy days of the year.

By three in the afternoon, the three of them were safely on board the luncheon cruise yacht. Colin had to chase Zackary around the two open main decks, as the boy zoomed into and around corners in his wheelchair. All the while Jill and Sarah just looked on with a soothing sense of contentment and relief. Their family unit had reunited and old wounds were now safely healing. But as Colin and Zach were dashing around, there were two puzzling oddities Colin couldn't help but notice.

The first was that on the aft deck there was a very large trunk snuggled up against the exterior dining room cabin wall. It seemed somehow out of place, even though it was painted entirely white with the traditional Red Cross on its top and sides. However, it had a double lock on it, both of which appeared to be somewhat complicated for someone to open in a time of crisis. And the second was that he had observed three oddly dressed individuals either around it or peering from the interior of the dining room out on to it. And there was something odd about how each was dressed. It was like some ceremonial garb. But given the festive mood of their day, he quickly dismissed it as probably being something to do with a particular religion or sect's way of observing the holidays. And yet, if he had time before they got underway, he'd like to ask one of the cabin crew why the emergency gear was so securely locked, but soon the thought was dismissed in the rush to catch up with Zackary. But equally odd, he had seen no one in traditional cabin crew attire…only these few individuals dressed strangely and the other tourists who looked pretty much like he and his family.

At about the same time, across the eastern border of France, E.B., Joan and Elliot had become well settled in Base Housing at the Ramstein Air Base. Being there for almost a year by December, 2012, they had ample time to have camping trips along the Rhine River and up and down the Moselle River. The area around Trier was their favorite spot to return to; it was close enough to the Base to visit or spend the night if they wanted to.

And E.B.'s duty was perfect for what Joan and he had hoped it might provide... a break from combat and from the hectic world of training other pilots. All he flew now was a desk. And they both agreed that upon the end of this tour of duty, he would resign from the Army and return home to Fort Davis. Joan's calm and all-knowing love had begun to work its magic and the dancing E.B. was starting to perform was transforming more and more away from the cultural and international wars that raged everywhere. His inoculation against ritualized manhood status was nearly complete. In its place was evolving a simpler person, one who wanted to protect his loved ones, but not out of rage, anger or a sense of inferiority.

As a final reward regarding his service, given that his enlistment term would be over come January 31, 2013, just little over a month away, his brigade commander gave him a week's pass to drive over to Paris for the Christmas Holiday. They were to leave on December 19th and return on the 26th.

Elliot, in particular, was ecstatic when his dad told him. As part of E.B.'s incorporation into his family, he had to accept and understand that his son was not like himself... the rather rugged, independent-minded boy raised on a ranch in West Texas. Elliot already fancied a much different style and approach, and he adored his mother far beyond anything E.B. had ever done or seen, even with his sisters' relationship to his mom. His precious son, along with his indescribably wonderful mother, was the treasure of his life, and because of that, whatever his son cared for or about and however he expressed that enthusiasm was just fine with him. His dance steps were now getting closer and closer to what could be described as tap dancing.

Happy and relieved, Joan, Elliot and E.B. climbed into their somewhat modified off-road, all-wheeled drive jeep, one that each of them agreed would be shipped back to the States when they resettled at the © Ranch in Fort Davis, and took the most direct highway from the Base into France, passing through Metz on their way into Paris. They had made prior reservations in a small, reasonably-priced hotel in the Montmartre District of Paris, where they could just park their jeep and take the subway or bus wherever they wanted to go. And they covered the city top to bottom in the days before Christmas Eve. Even the snow the couple of days before then didn't slow them down. The City was theirs. It was a joyous time, and to cap it off, at Joan's insistence, they planned to end their week of sightseeing at the Isle de la Cite come mid-afternoon on Christmas Eve.

Their arrival there was such a relief. For the first time during their week's stay, they had gotten mixed up on which subway train to take and had ended up in the Bios de Boulogne. So they arrived at the plaza in front of the Notre Dame Cathedral later than expected. It was 4:15 p.m. and dusk was gathering, as was a huge crowd to celebrate Christmas.

Eager to see the Seine from the vantage point of the massive plaza, the family ran over to the quay to look down at the river, then around to the various bridges and out toward the vista of the Eiffel Tower in the distance. It was a glorious sight. But just as they were about to turn away, E.B. noticed something going on below them, on the deck of a rather fancy yacht moored there. Becoming more than just curious, he called out to Joan and Elliot who had strolled a ways further down the wall, "Give me a second, I'm going to slip down and see what's happening on the boat apparently secured to the dock below here…"

Inti, on the other hand, did not have just a holiday celebration in mind when he was making the final arrangements for a yacht to be reserved for Christmas Eve. If all went as planned, it would be a historic surprise for all of Paris and beyond.

THE COLLISION

SIXTEEN: FINAL PREPARATION

The other three members of al Haboob left on November 1st, with the package that been stored at a secure military facility near Fordo. A small military convoy accompanied them as they drove down to the port of Bandar Abbäs located on the Strait of Hormuz. From there, they were to guard and to insure that the very heavy, oversized and double locked container was placed onboard an oversized fishing vessel, one of many which use this ancient city as a home port. It had to be hoisted aboard using the crane usually reserved for lifting nets full of tuna up on the dock when the fishing fleet arrived back at home port. Few, other than a new crew and three others who seemed to direct all the handling of the large cargo, were in the area late that night when it was finally loaded on board the vessel.

For anyone who had been familiar with this ship's regular crew, they would have been puzzled to see that the well-protected crate that was not being crewed by the usual crewmembers on this voyage. None of the usual crew appeared to be anywhere in the vicinity or on board.

Instead, the crew appeared to be young men of military age and appearance, similar to the three others who were dressed completely in black. Unbeknownst to anyone but the other two dressed in black, one of the three slunk away for a flight to Marseille, France, after the package was loaded.

Once the fishing vessel cleared the port's breakwater on November 10th, it headed south and then east into the Gulf of Oman, the Arabian Sea, Gulf of Aden, Red Sea and up the Gulf of Suez into the Suez Canal into the Mediterranean Sea. Its destination was Cerbère, a small fishing and resort village, the farthest point on the southern coast of France. It is east of Marseille and far from the peering eyes of custom agents and the more aggressive investigative skills of the federal police; eachl on alert for incoming boats smuggling drugs, contraband... and worse.

Given the unpredictable weather changes associated with the transition from Fall to Winter, the trip, although calm in the Gulf of Oman and the Arabian Sea and of course through the Suez Canal, was nothing of the kind once they cleared land out of Port Said, Egypt. Navigation across the sea to the coast of France was at times almost terrifying for the crew, each active duty Iranian navy sailors. And the two cohorts of Inti left aboard were seasick the entire crossing. As much as they were supposed to insure that their container they hoisted on board was secure and safe, none of them ventured below to the hold throughout that phase of the journey. Earlier zeal had been replaced by continuous nausea and vomiting. The coastline of France couldn't come sooner in view for each of them.

And on the evening of November 29th, the lights of the Cerbère Harbor appeared on the horizon. Now all the two companions of the package had to do was call their contact that had flown to Marseille and was supposed to arrange for a bobtail rental truck with a hydraulic lift gate to come to the outer portion of the harbor's ancient stone wharf. In the darkness later that night the entire crew would carefully unload the container onto the dock and then lift it onto the lift gate to be raised high enough to be shifted inside the truck. Speed and stealth were absolutely vital at this crucial point in transporting the cargo. Failure here would doom the nearly year-long process of planning and preparation.

And as fortune or destiny would have it, they had it unloaded and the large fishing vessel on the way within an hour of its docking. The truck was waiting with its engine idling throughout the transfer. Once the crate was secured inside the truck, two deliverers jumped into the cab and the other one melted into the town's shadows. And over the next week both the truck and two other members of al Haboob made their way to Paris; the truck traveling the highway to Perpignan, Carcassone, Toulouse, Bordeaux, Tours, Orlèans and finally into the outskirts of Paris, where the two not traveling in the truck had arranged a garage with an apartment overhead for all of them and the cargo to hide.

Meanwhile, Inti had blossomed into a serious secret agent for changing the status quo… or at least that was the rationale that now dominated his thinking. Revenge and chaos might have more accurately described his motivation, as the months turned into weeks and then into only days before the plan of the al Haboob unfolded fully. The time had come for him to ask the all-important favor of his and Froncett's now frequent companion at various social events and parties: the Minister of the Interior. They had all become quite chummy, and Inti had discussed a couple of times about charting the Minister's yacht for a combined private and limited public cruise on the Seine. Finally he broached the critical question; could he arrange to charter the "le Lointain Horizon", for an afternoon luncheon cruise on the Seine for Christmas Eve?

And to his absolute relief, the Minister said he would gladly arrange it all and then asked if he could possibly be a guest as well.

It was perfect. Arrangements were made to have the boat tied up at the dock southwest of the Eiffel Tower by noon that day. It would then be stocked and ready to begin receiving luncheon guests by 2 p.m. and later be launched for a four hour tour and meal by 3 p.m.

Coincidentally, it was about the same day that Inti got this news about the yacht that he got a text message on the cell phone that he had been given when he left Iran but was told to never use it and yet keep it fully charged and turned on during the day. When he did get the message, he was to call the number indicated when it was safe and secure for him to do so.

And on December 18th, he got the text message, as he was leaving the Fajr prayer, the first day's prayer at The Mosque. Looking around casually, he saw an empty and isolated roadside bench, which he walked over to and sat down. Within a few more minutes, after scanning the area for any onlookers, he tapped in the text message numbers he had just been sent. .

"How are you Inti", the familiar voice of Jon asked.

"Well, and yourself?"

"Everything is here and in order", came the reply, succinct enough and yet indicating that their months-long effort was about to become a reality. "Do you have any details for me?"

"Yes.   Be at Pier 36 at 12:30 p.m. on the 24th, everyone will begin arriving around 2 p.m. and launch time is at 3 p.m.   I would expect the 'gift' should be opened around 4 p.m. once we dock briefly adjacent to Notre Dame."

"Perfect." was Jon's only reply, and the phone went dead. And just before Inti stood, he quickly dismantled the cell phone and placed different pieces of it in various trash bins as he walked back to his family's apartment.

The time was at hand. Now all that had to be done at his end was to insure that everyone invited was given the 2 p.m. boarding time and the yacht's location. Everything else would be up to Jon and his crew. Once he got to the ship, it was prearranged that Jon would give him the new phone, the one to be used to send the triggering, coded message.

SEVENTEEN: DANCE MACREBA

Occasionally, we are allowed enough time to restart our dance routines years before our final curtain call. And sometimes there are only moments... even just seconds to allow that opportunity to display the performance that we would like to be remembered by. Too often the dance routine is permanently imprinted at a young age, and no deviation or alteration is allowed or permitted. Such is the case with most manhood rituals. With these rituals, any dance partners chosen will likely be disrespected or rarely cherished or truly loved; there can be no experimenting with other dance steps offering a better life; there will be little or no music; and there most often will be nothing but a drum beat of boots steadily marching in cadence, seeking conquest after conquest. It is often the only or the final dance that so much of humanity has known for far too long, and it was about to start being performed out again come 12:30 p.m. on December 24th, 2012.

As the bobtail truck appeared at the dock next to the "le Lointain Horizon", its regular crew was busy setting tables and cooking the sumptuous late luncheon meal below deck. The engineer was below as well, making all the usual safety and mechanical checks before the cruise began. He was anxious, as were all the crew members, to get this party on its way and get back here, so they could go home to their families for the Christmas Eve celebrations. There was a heightened sense of expectation, and most of the crew was humming or whistling when the five individuals dressed in colorful Middle East-looking garb walked into the yacht's cabin.

Looking up, the cabin steward, calmly glanced over and politely said, "I'm sorry, we will not beginning boarding until 2 p.m.; would you please mind waiting outside until…." and then two muffled shots rang out, and he dropped to the floor. And with the expertise and efficiency of a perfectly coordinated, elite military unit, the five new arrivals dispersed through the yacht and efficiently disposed of each of the boat's crewmembers.

And while three of the al Haboob quickly spirited the bodies down into a far corner of the engine room and covered them with a tarp, two others went back to the waiting truck and opened the tail gate and climbed in to move the oversized trunk back onto the lift gate to be lowered to the ground. By now the container had been painted pure white with the universal insignia of the Red Cross painted on its top and sides. And while the crate was being moved into place on the truck's tailgate, one of the three members of the team still on the yacht, moved a couple of aft deck chairs inside the cabin, making room for the white container to rest against the exterior wall of the dining room.

All five then placed canvas straps under the container and moved it off the lift ramp once it was lowered to the ground. Next, they struggled to move it down the ramp onto the aft deck, and positioned it snugly against the cabin's wall, just under the window. It was a perfect fit, no view was obstructed. It was their unanimous opinion that it would not attract much attention. And then each of them hurriedly began their preplanned jobs of resuming setting up for the luncheon and getting the engine room ready and food and drinks prepared.

At 2 p.m. the small gate at the head of the pedestrian ramp was opened allowing the dinner guests to board the yacht. First in line were Inti and his family, followed by about ten other invited guests and their families, including the Minister of the Interior and his family. Last to board was Colin and his family. He had been lucky enough to call ahead to schedule this cruise before they closed all reservations. As mentioned previously, this was to be the highlight of their holiday. And once the luncheon was finished, they would return to Notre Dame for the Christmas Eve service. Everyone was joyous and full of the spirit of Christmas. Paris was resplendent with her white cape of snow on the roof tops and a lowering sun giving the lengthening shadows a chance to accentuate her magnificent monuments of graceful architecture, quaint side streets and expansive parklands.

Almost immediately Zackary began wheeling excitedly around the deck, with Colin chasing after him. He giggled wildly as his dad exaggerated his calling out for him to slow down. There was pure glee in the boy's voice, and great satisfaction in Jill's mind that her family was at last fully enjoying and loving each other. She reached over and held Sarah, muttering, "It's so wonderful to have you here beside me, Sarah. You are so very precious to me." A smile spread over the young girl's face and she replied, "I love you and dad so very much."

And the race with Zachary continued until Colin

stopped to focus on the white trunk. It seemed oddly out of place and oversized, even if there were likely life vests inside it. And why would it be so heavily bolted. And then when he took the time to look around again and see the colorful dress of the yacht staff, his curiosity only increased. There was something about all this set up that didn't seem right. He had been on enough boats of various sizes on Queensland's Sunshine Coast as a boy to sense there was a mismatch; this vessel was not in shipshape condition. But it wasn't until the boat got underway at 3 p.m. that he became overly concerned. One of the first passengers who brought his wife, two older children and a baby seemed to hover continually around the trunk, as did two of the crew. They were trying too hard to not appear too obvious. And it almost appeared to Colin that some of the crew was actually guarding the oversized trunk.

However, he became distracted once the trip started, when Jill called out to him to see the remarkable parade of buildings and monuments pass in review as they motored quietly upstream. First there was the Eiffel Tower, followed by The Invalides and Grand Palais, the National Assembly building, the Louvre, and then on the left side of the river, after passing under many gracefully arched bridges, was the Notre Dame Cathedral. It was here that they were told the cruise would pick up the last passengers for their dinner, which would be served as soon as they left the dock.

It was when they docked that Inti caught Colin's immediate and undivided attention. His dark brown skin and broad nose and wide cheek bones did not conform to the immigrants that he had seen in London and here in Paris; all of whom he surmised were from the African continent somewhere. This individual appeared to be more

Mesoamerican or South American. And he appeared quite nervous and fidgety. From all appearances, it appeared that his wife was likewise upset over his behavior, because she kept running back and forth, in and out of the cabin onto the aft deck to speak to him. A couple of times they even appeared to be arguing, because once she stormed off. To Colin, for this individual to be the host for most of the passengers, he seemed far too distracted and nervous for his comfort.

And as they pulled up to the dock, about 3:30 p.m. Colin noticed the one confirming clue that plunged him into action: it was seeing a revolver inside the capes of the two individuals appearing to guard the large white box. When he saw these, he turned to Jill and said, "Sit tight. There is something I need to check out. And if it isn't to my liking we are getting off the boat as soon as I get back."

And without Jill having a chance to ask, both he and Froncett rushed simultaneously onto the aft deck. In her case, she had had it with Inti's rudeness with the invited guests. He'd spent no time with them since they left the quay at the Eiffel Tower. And he had been downright rude to her the last time she spoke to him about this.

As the two were moving toward Inti, the two individuals who were guarding the box were joined by two of the other crew, dressed the same way, and they began trying to restrain both Colin and Froncett.

Then the shouting started, with Colin yelling, "Why do those two men have revolvers in side holsters?!! Who are they?!! Who are all of you?"!!!

And it was at this point that E.B. leaned over the ledge had looked down and saw the commotion going on. Turning to Joan and Elliot he said, "Hold on a minute. I see someone who may need help down there on that boat."

And he quickly spun around and rushed down the ancient stone ramp onto the pier where le Lointain Horizon had just moored. Leaping over the shallow side rail, not waiting for the little gate to open, E.B. rushed faster and faster toward the mounting confrontation at the stern of the yacht. And it was just before he got there that Inti pulled out his cell phone and began pounding a password on its keys.

At that moment, Colin seeing both the phone and Inti's nervous hammering out some message, knew something terrible was about to happen. It was an all-knowing moment, as he screamed, "STOP HIM!! THERE'S A BOMB ON BOARD THIS BOAT!!!"

Hearing this just a second or two before he came upon the screaming and scuffling group, E.B. leaped, as did Colin, and the two of them collided into Inti, as he typed out the last letter of "Allähu Akbar!" ("God is Great!").

And within a millisecond of that completed message, there was a tearing sound, as if the earth's surface was being ripped apart by some cosmic force. It signaled the splitting of particles, sub particles, atoms, electrons, basic elements and the total destruction of the City of Light. There was a simultaneous screaming noise so high pitched and intense that whatever initial injury or vaporization occurred subsequently, no sense of hearing was left intact throughout the city at that moment. There then followed a light so brilliant, so intense that it imbedded itself onto and into anything left standing for miles and miles in all directions. Whatever remained was coated with whiteness mixed with the blackened remains of rubble. Then following the immense burst of light, there was a horrific bursting-forth roar, a sound so loud that it had always been buried deep within the fears and nightmares of anyone born in the latter twentieth century up to that day. The most terrifying event imaginable was erupting in one of humanities most beloved cities. And confirming that this was indeed happening, springing forth out of this eruption of fire and death was the long-dreaded voice of the genie. Its harrowing bellow, shrieked across the mortally wounded city as it left its confines. Death directed solely at all humanity was being unleashed as never before, and its thunderous howl preceded by milliseconds the force of its explosive power that was next to come. The blast itself followed.

And for six-tenths of a mile in all directions from that dockside mooring of the le Lointain Horizon, there was nothing recognizable left. Nothing. Everything in that radius was swept off the face of the planet by the force of the explosion.   Gone were the marvelous chapels, cathedrals, museums, bridges and most importantly… countless lives, unsung songs, yet to be performed dances and dreams and hopes for renewal and rebirth.   All vanished forever. And left instead was a crater 200 feet deep and 1,000 feet in diameter, one that was steadily being filled with churning, debris and corpse-filled water of the Seine flowing blindly downstream in and around the remains of Paris.

For one and seven tenths miles from the blast's origin, ninety percent of the city's population was killed. Wind speeds exceeding 300 miles per hour were experienced in this radius. It was a killing zone like no one could have or ever wanted to conceive.

And up to two and seven tenths miles from the blast's epicenter, fifty percent of the population was killed and 40% were injured.   All but the most reinforced buildings were leveled as well in this zone.

Yet, even with all this destruction and countless dead and dying, the death toll was to rise much higher for up to 90 miles in all directions due to the lethal doses of radiation released by this well designed and constructed 1 megaton hydrogen bomb. (see Appendix: **The Destruction of Paris**).

The dance of death had triumphed. The rituals of manhood succeeded over the attempts of some to learn a new kind of dance, one that allowed them to be simply a man. This day was a replay of a scenario seen... on a lesser scale to be sure... too often in the course of human history. And from December 24th, 2012 forward, the forces of retribution and revenge worldwide pushed aside even further the desire of too few to begin their lives and dancing anew.

THE DANCING ENDS

EPILOGUE

Despite the two decades that have passed since this earth-shattering tragedy, I now fully realize that it is impossible to know everything that is necessary to explain how (and most importantly why) this destruction of Paris happened. Why, for instance, did Inti become so transformed into a zealot, sacrificing a career that would have undoubtedly resulted in a Nobel Laureate in Physics nomination? How could his wife, Froncett, not know that something of utter madness was afoot by his behavior and activities? Why did his family mean so little to him that he would slaughter them as well? For what?... for his place with the supposedly ridiculously touted harem of virgins in the hereafter? Does total annihilation offer the only hope and meaning to these fanatical killers? They are, after all, nothing more than that. The six individuals who were assisted, fed, housed, transported and given every possible manner of help to accomplish their twisted idea of justice, as well as a fruitless and suicidal avenue to total control and a delusional and maniacal promise of conversion through the overt support and blessing of a sovereign state were all guilty of the most serious crime against humanity ever perpetrated in one event.

What do you do about those equally responsible for this horrible act? Annihilate an entire country? Region? What does it take to live in peace? To have harmony? Are we, in actual fact, a species doomed to always battle each other, until finally using these horrific weapons makes our entire existence and that of all life on this planet extinct? Is that the ultimate goal? Extinction?

And what if Colin and my brother had been able to stop this event from occurring? What if they could have overpowered the guards, tossed the cell phone into the Seine before the code had fully activated the bomb? What if those Ministers had become suspicious of someone becoming so ingratiating? And most damning of all, what if the dances that mankind so obviously gravitates toward did not appear to invariably lead to the dance of death, the Dance Macabre? What if these silly, but all-important rituals of manhood were ridiculed, abolished and transformed into something so much more meaningful and truly caring?

This entire idea of manhood and its associated rituals have been defining the roles that men have had to conform to for eons. Each boy has to eventually decide whether he was to be the impregnator, the provider and/or the protector. And they had to do so in an acceptable fashion, through rituals that were and are nothing more than cultic or mystical trappings of a distant and brutal past.

Why shouldn't all males, and for that matter, us females, be defined not by the roles that are supposedly predestined for us by questionable cultural traditions and expectations, but instead by the qualities of character we bring to a society, those of caring, loving, wisdom, strength, originality, steadfastness, dependability, faithfulness, trustworthiness, reverence and goodness?

I have been surrounded by tragedy and heartache for years and years... ever since this horror struck our civilization. On that day in December, 2012, over two million people lost their lives almost immediately. And another million have died in France alone in the months and years that followed due to the bomb's aftereffects.

My job and passion have been to study the bits of recording tape, satellite surveillance photos, videos, photographs, testimonials, bills of lading, transcripts, letters, telephone messages, fingerprints and government documents domestic and foreign ever since that awful day in December, 2012. I left my job and took on another one to do so. It became my sole mission in life to uncover as much of what and why this event occurred. And I have only two conclusions, amongst countless unanswered questions that will undoubtedly never be answered satisfactorily.

One is that my take on all this is that only by the world adopting dancing and more specifically, the spirit of Tap Dancing, can we go forward as a civilization. Certainly, you might say this dance is being used as a metaphor for the measure of a decently lived life. And to some extent that is true; there is a balance to using it as an approach to daily life. And while it is usually performed by a single individual; it can only be perfected further by a couple performing it together. Then it has a beauty, skill and grace far beyond what one performer can showcase. It is then the music and real dancing begins.

There are snares, traps and sharp objects all along the way in life. They are all part of learning this dance. Through learning it you maneuver around and through them with a grace, poise and determination. The reward is that you have a musical accompaniment throughout this journey, and you can easily choose to have a partner, who dances her or his own steps independently of yours, but still in unison and concert as well. It becomes a true partnership of learning and commitment. It can become adapted and continually perfected. It radiates a happiness and joy like none other. It adapts to different music. It is bold; it holds back nothing. It demands concentration, practice and self-sacrifice. And, most important, there is nothing enigmatic associated with it; you see, hear and feel it as it is.

Most importantly, there can be no music or beauty in any dance as long as the traditional method and ritual of achieving the mythical goal of manhood is the objective. The lives of Inti, Colin and my brother demonstrate this most vividly. Each of them was a victim of this approach, but Colin and my brother were struggling hard to free themselves from it at the end of their lives.

And to conclude, my second and final comment is that becoming a man has been an enigma throughout most of human history. Too often it has been melded into or simply confused with the rite of passage into so-called manhood. The distinction could not be clearer. One is a fabrication of each society... large or small... with beliefs, rituals and emotions that invariably lead to the worst of times, if left unchecked. The other comprises qualities of character, which are the very essence of one's God-given soul. The former too often led and still leads neighborhoods, States, countries... even civilizations... into strife, conflict and destruction. The latter channels men into living in harmony and peace with all that is around them. But, tragically, how rare have been those moments; for themselves, for their spouses, for their families and for much of the world around them.

At some point, enough men must come forward and shout in one voice to others around them to stop the killing, cease the needless anger and the groundless suspicion and halt continually performing the dances that only lead to mistrust and hate. One day this must come to pass. And then beginning on that day mankind will no longer be the enigma that has tormented the very soul of every civilization, since before the beginning of recorded time.

It is my only prayer this day that the necessary changes will begin now. They most certainly must begin now... Let the dancing begin anew. Usher your partner out onto the dance floor. The music is about to begin...

Signed,

Nin Corwin
Investigative Agent
Federal Bureau of Investigation
Washington, D.C.

APPENDIX

1.   Guanay, Bolivia:

2.   The Bolivia Yungas Road (The Road of Death):

3.   La Paz, Bolivia:

↓ Mt. Illamani

4. The Glasshouse Mountains:
Landsborough ↓  → Caloundra

---

5. University of Queensland St. Lucia Campus, Brisbane, Queensland:

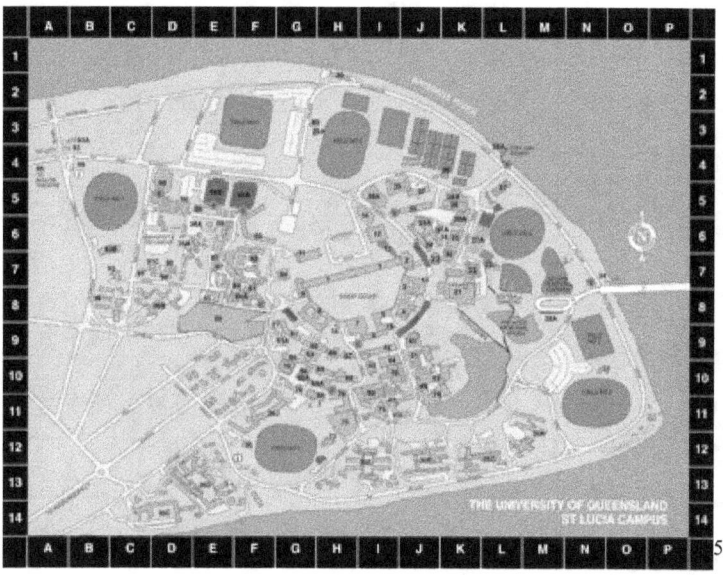

6. Colin Clark Building (School of Economics, Business and Law):

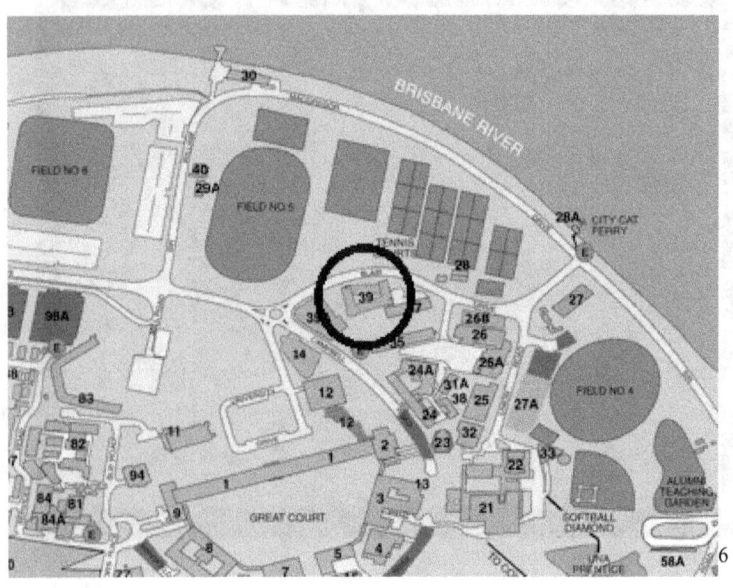

---

[6] Used with permission from Thomas Joyce (t.joyce@library.uq.edu.au)

7. Colin Kennard's Bachelor of Economics (BEcon) Three Year Curriculum:

Year One

Course Code	Units	Course Title
First Semester		
ACCT1101	2	Accounting for Decision Making
ECON1010	2	Introductory Microeconomics
ECON1020	2	Introductory Macroeconomics
ECON1050	2	Tools of Economic Analysis
Second Semester		
ECON1310	2	Quantitative Economic & Business Analysis A
ECON2020	2	Macroeconomic Theory
ECON2040	2	Macroeconomic Policy
ECON2300	2	Introductory Econometrics

Year Two

First Semester		
ECON1320	2	Quantitative Economic &

		Business Analysis B
ECON2110	2	Political Economy & Comparative Systems
ECON2560	2	Globalization & Economic Development
ECON2050	2	Mathematical Economics

Second Semester

ECON2510	2	Development Economics
ECON2540	2	Economics of Innovation & Entrepreneurship
ECON2610	2	International Economy in the Twentieth Century
ECON3330	2	Econometric Theory

Year Three
(Major Declared in International Trade & Finance)

First Semester

ECON2200	2	Management of Financial Institutions (mandatory)
ECON3610	2	International Trade Theory & Policy
ECON2500	2	China: Emergence, Implications &

		Challenges
ECON3020	2	Advanced Macroeconomics
ECON3520	2	International Macroeconomics

Second Semester

ECON3200	2	Monetary Economics
ECON3210	2	Financial Markets & Institutions
ECON3350	2	Applied Econometrics for Macroeconomics & Finance
ECON3550	2	Economic Institutions & Global Banking
ECON3403	2	International Financial Management[7]

---

[7] Used with permission from Thomas Joyce (t.joyce@library.uq.edu.au)

8. Frontier Forts of Texas:

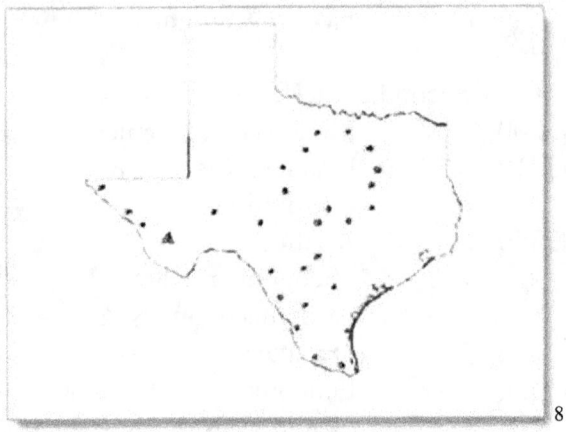

♠ Fort Davis, 1854.

---

[8] Adapted from reference material found in the <u>Texas Almanac-2004-2005</u>, Published by the Dallas Morning News.

9. Fort Davis:

[9] Photograph used with permission from Anne at the Fort Davis Chamber of Commerce, www.fortdavis.com.

10. Fort Davis, Texas; Corwin Ranch Location and Fort Davis:

Corwin Ranch ↓   ↓Fort Davis, Texas   ↓Fort Davis

---

[10] Photograph used with permission from Rick Gutleber, the photographer. Please note this image had to be changed to black and white for publication. In full color, it is an elegant photograph. It can be found on Flickr.com under the heading of Fort Davis, Texas.

11. Map of Paris:

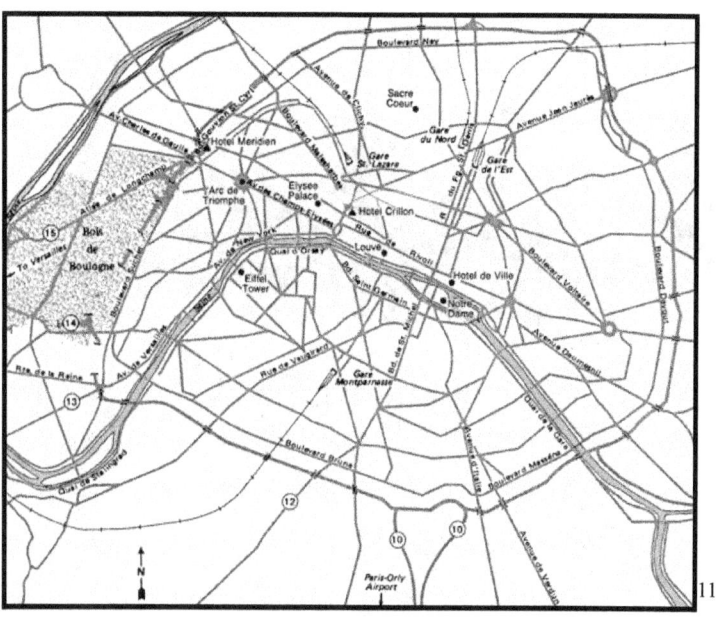

---

12. Kew Gardens station with various business adjacent to it:

[12] Wikimedia Commons. Photo taken byPatche99z on March 114, 2007. Taken from Wikipedia.

13. Colin and Jill's Tudor Revival Home:

(No citations could be found for this image. Unfortunately, as a result, no credit can be given or permission asked for its usage. The author sincerely apologizes for any oversight this may cause.)

14. AH-64 Army Apache Helicopter:

13

---
13 Image is in the Public Domain, as it was taken by a U.S. Army
soldier or a U.S. federal government employee. Taken from
Wikipedia.

15. Haboob:

16. The Destruction of Paris:

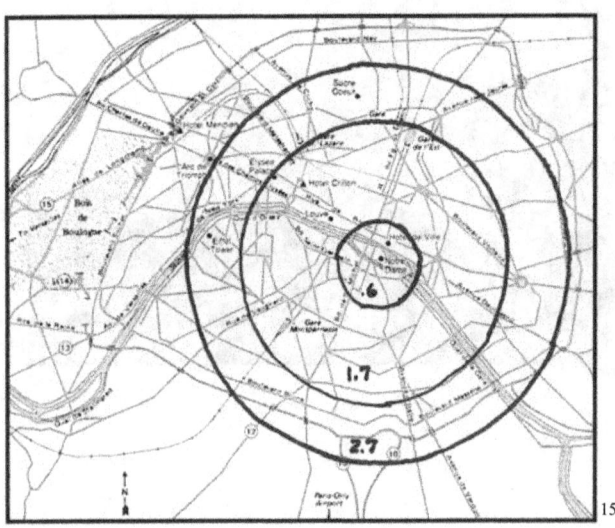

[15] This is a royalty free map of Paris, France. Adapted by this book's author.

REFERENCES

1. Manhood in the Making- Cultural Concepts of Masculinity, David D. Gilmore. Yale University Press, New Haven, 1990.
2. Manhood in America- A Cultural History, Michael Kimmel. The Free Press, New York, 1996.
3. Texas Almanac-2004-2005, Elizabeth Cruce Alvarez, Editor. The Dallas Morning News, Dallas, 2004.
4. London-The Green Guide, Alison Coupe, Editor. Michelin Apa Publications, Ltd., London, 2010.
5. Paris-The Green Guide, Manufacture française des pneumatiques Michelin, Belgium, 2001.
6. Germany-West Germany and Berlin, Manufacture française des pneumatiques Michelin, France, 1982.
7. Wikipedia, The Free Encyclopedia: Warrant Officer, Shria Law, Education in Bolivia, Education in Australia, Bolivian Food, Bolivia, Altiplano, Schinus molle, Leo (astrology), The University of Queensland, Paris, University of Paris, Iran, Pakistan, Muslim Brotherhood, 1st Cavalry.
8. Guyland-The Perilous World Where Boys Become Men, Michael Kimmel. Harper Collins, New York, 2008.
9. Meanings for Manhood-Constructions of Masculinity in Victorian America, Edited by Mark C. Carnes and Clyde Griffen. The University of Chicago Press, Chicago, 1990.
10. Missing from Action, Weldon M. Hardenbrook. Thomas Nelson Publishers, Nashville, 1987.
11. Manhood For Amateurs-The Pleasures and Regrets of a Husband, Father and Son, Michael Chabon. Harper Luxe, New York, 2009.

12. <u>Manhood of Humanity</u>, 2nd edition, Alfred
    Korzybski.The International Non-Aristotelian
    Library Publishing Co., Lakeville, Conn., 1950.
13. <u>The Last Utopia-Human Rights in History</u>, Samuel
    Moyn. The Belknap Press of Harvard University
    Press, Cambridge, 2010.
14. "The Effects of Nuclear War", Washington Office of
    Technology Assessment, Congress of the United
    States, May, 1979.
15. A survey done in April, 2011, by individual men and
    couples who epitomize the best of what it means to
    be a man. They were all residents at Cougar Springs
    Senior Living Community in Redmond, Oregon.